Grandpa's smile seemed to make his dark eyes twinkle.

"You'd better talk to your grandma about winning over a woman's heart."

"What's this?" Grandma came in with a tall glass of tea.

"Will needs our help, Betty."

She sat down and placed her hands in her lap. "You got ten minutes. Cookies are in the oven."

Will laughed. "Tell me how to win Taylor. She thinks our time has passed. Too late. Lost what we once had."

Grandma waved her hand. "Taylor's easy, Will. She already loves you. I can see it in her eyes. You just need to let her know that no matter what, you're going to be there for her. Never let her go. Prove whatever happened between you ten years ago won't happen again."

Will grinned. Simple. Wise. Brilliant. Hopefully, not impossible.

RACHEL HAUCK lives in Florida with her husband, Tony, a youth pastor. A graduate of Ohio State University, she worked for seventeen years in the software industry before leaving to write and work in ministry. She is also a speaker and worship leader. Rachel served the writing community as president of American Christian Fiction Writers. Visit her Web site at www.rachelhauck.com.

Books by Rachel Hauck

HEARTSONG PRESENTS
HP574—Lambert's Pride with Lynn A. Coleman
HP661—Lambert's Code

Lambert's Peace

Rachel Hauck

Heartsong Presents

For Jesus, the Christ, the Prince of Peace.

A note from the Author:
I love to hear from my readers! You may correspond with me by writing:

Rachel Hauck
Author Relations
PO Box 721
Uhrichsville, OH 44683

ISBN 1-59310-847-8

LAMBERT'S PEACE

All scripture quotations are taken from the King James Version of the Bible.

Our mission is to publish and distribute inspirational products offering exceptional value and biblical encouragement to the masses.

PRINTED IN THE U.S.A.

one

Taylor Hanson parked her new BMW in the shade of her childhood home, pressed her head against the steering wheel, and whispered a prayer.

Lord, what have I done?

After a moment, she drew a long breath, smoothed her hands down the front of her dark red linen suit, and popped the BMW's trunk. Stepping out of the car and into the afternoon light, she wondered how many times she'd driven the familiar roads from Manhattan to White Birch and back again.

Gold-tipped maple leaves rustled in the afternoon breeze as she yanked her suitcases from the car's trunk and slung the strap of her laptop case over her shoulder, then snapped the trunk shut.

Any other day, any other time, the beauty of the day would motivate her to change her clothes and go for a good, long run. But for now, in this moment, her heart remained locked in the dark places of disappointment, frustration, and anxiety.

As she walked toward the kitchen door, dragging her suitcases behind, Taylor pinched her lips together, determined not to cry.

She did this to herself. She'd calculated the cost and acted. Nevertheless, she never imagined *this* would happen to her.

Taylor entered the two-story brick home and called, "Mom?"

No answer. The house was quiet and perfumed with the lingering scent of bread and cinnamon.

Taylor lugged her suitcases up the back stairs from the kitchen to her old bedroom. She dropped her designer purse and laptop case onto her worn oak desk, shoved her luggage and overnight bag against the wall, then fell face-first into the familiar comfort of her old bed.

Lord, please tell me I didn't ruin my life. She sat up with a jerk, pressing her fingers against her eyes.

"Get ahold of yourself, Taylor." She paced around her old room. "This is a minor setback."

She removed her laptop from its monogrammed leather case, booted it up, and hooked up to the phone line. While dialing out to the World Wide Web, Taylor made a note in her electronic data assistant: *Arrange for broadband Internet connection at Mom and Dad's*. She would need it.

For the rest of the morning and afternoon, Taylor surfed the Web, made calls, and e-mailed contacts. She barely noticed when the afternoon light faded to the muted colors of dusk and dark shadows fell across her room.

When a thin, familiar "Hello?" sounded down the hall, she glanced up from the computer.

"Mom, in here."

Trixie Hanson graced the doorway and flipped on the light. "Taylor, what are you doing here?"

Taylor gave her mom a hug. The petite, trig woman wore a navy suit with matching pumps. "How are you?"

"Fine; exhausted. I've been at a ladies' aid meeting for the church bazaar."

"Ladies' aid meeting? Can Mrs. Cramer still talk a mannequin to death?"

Mom smiled. "Of course. Some things never change; you know that. But never mind about Dot—what are you doing home? It's the middle of the week."

In the faint glow of the lamp's light, Taylor saw the concerned expression on her mother's delicate features.

"I just needed to come home." She sat on the edge of her bed, realizing she still wore her business suit and two-inch heels. Her makeup felt stale and congealed, and the idea of a shower reminded her of how good the community pool felt on a hot summer day.

Mom studied her for a moment. "Are you all right?"

Taylor kicked off her shoes and squished her toes into the carpet nap. "I'm fine. Is this carpet new?"

"Yes, it is." Mom studied her for a moment then added, "And it is highly unusual for you to show up unannounced, Taylor. Are you sure everything is all right?"

"Well, I'm not sick or hurt, if that's what you mean." Taylor opened one of her suitcases, looking for a pair of jeans and a T-shirt. She wanted to explain her sudden appearance in White Birch but still had trouble understanding the events of the last three days herself.

"Hello. . .anybody home? Trixie?"

Mom fluttered over to the doorway. "Grant. Up here in Taylor's room."

In few seconds, Dad's cheery face peered around the door. "My two favorite women." He kissed Trixie and wrapped his arms around Taylor.

"So," he started, holding her at arm's length, "what are you doing home?" His gray eyes sparkled with merriment.

Sadness washed over Taylor like a chilling waterfall. How could she tell her biggest fan—the man who had dubbed her the whiz kid—that she'd failed?

"Taylor, is everything all right?"

She said without rehearsal, "I left Blankenship and Burns."

Trixie leaned on Grant's arm. "What do you mean?"

"I quit." She hated the sound of that word—*quit*. It spelled failure.

Grant chuckled. "She's teasing us, Trixie."

Taylor peered into her father's eyes. "No, Daddy, I'm not. Movers are packing up my apartment as we speak. I'm putting my stuff in storage." She glanced around her room. "I'd like to stay here for a while if I could."

Mom gasped and covered her cheek with her hand. "Really, Taylor. You actually quit. Well, I never—"

Taylor snapped. "Yes, Mom, I quit." Grant held up his hands. "Okay, you two, let's go down and have some hot tea and some of Mom's coffee cake. Then, Taylor, you can fill us in."

❧

Will Adams sat on the edge of the couch in his twin brother's spacious living room. A blind date. What was he thinking?

"I'm thirty-three," he muttered, running his hand along the back of his neck. "Going on a blind date like a desperate schoolboy."

"Come on, it's not that bad," Bobby said, laughing. Will stood to pace, jiggling the keys in his pocket. "I can't believe I let you and Elle set me up."

"Beats sitting at home on a Friday night with Harry."

Will turned to him. "Harry's great company. Man's best friend, you know."

"It's one night, Will. One night. Who knows? You just might fall in love."

They were to pick Mia Wilmington up on their way to dinner at Italian Hills, the town's most romantic restaurant. Not Will's idea for a first date. Wouldn't a casual night of eating pizza at Giuseppe's be much better?

"You know, you're making this way harder than it has to be," Bobby said, glancing over his shoulder at Will while clicking through the sports channels. "You run a multimillion-dollar furniture company."

"Furniture, I know. Mia Wilmington, I don't," Will said, laughing softly as he regarded the man whose features mirrored his own.

Elle entered the room. "The kids are settled in the family room with your mom, fried chicken, and cold sodas."

The men stood. "You look beautiful, Elle." Bobby kissed his willowy wife.

Will slipped on his tan sports coat. "Let's go before I change my mind."

Elle brushed her hand down his arm. "Give tonight a chance, Will. It's been so long since you—"

Bobby interrupted. "Don't go there, Elle. He'll bite your head off." He held his wife's coat for her.

Elle slipped her arms into the sleeves. "I know it's hard to meet new people, Will."

"People I can handle. Blind dates. . .different species."

Elle exhaled. "Honestly, if I'd known it would traumatize you this much I wouldn't have bothered."

Will squirmed. Elle deserved more from him. "I'm sorry."

She linked her arm with his. "Don't worry, it's going to be wonderful."

On the ride to Mia's apartment, Elle reminded Will that his date taught performing arts at White Birch High School, possessed a very gregarious and bubbly personality, and had the "most beautiful smile."

Her words did little ease to Will's disdain for the situation, but he only had himself to blame. He'd said yes. Never again. Bobby had made a good point earlier. Will ran a multimillion-dollar company. He didn't need his sister-in-law to find him dates.

Walking alone to Mia's door, Will secretly hoped she wouldn't answer. But after one subtle knock, the door jerked open.

"You must be Will." A petite blond with deep-set green eyes stood in the doorway.

"I am."

She threw her arms around him. "I'm so happy to meet you."

Surprised, Will stumbled backward. "Nice to meet you, too." She tossed her head back, flipping long, straight blond hair over her shoulders. "Elle was right; you are handsome." She flashed Will a sparkling smile.

He shifted from one foot to the next. "Ready to go?"

"Absolutely," she said like she owned the word.

At Bobby's Volvo, Mia glided into the backseat, greeting Bobby and Elle.

Will shut her door and hurried around to the other side. Though she'd overwhelmed him at first, he found her extremely beautiful. Maybe this evening wouldn't be so bad after all.

Fifteen minutes later they were seated in the glow of flickering candles at Italian Hills, listening to the stringed music of the Merewether Quartet. They waved hello to their cousin Ethan's wife, Julie, the quartet's cellist.

They ordered iced teas and appetizers, and Mia chatted endlessly. She went from describing the day's school lunch to a pair of shoes she wanted to wear tonight but couldn't find.

Will watched closely to see if she took a breath between sentences.

When their server arrived with the appetizers, Mia placed her hand on Elle's shoulder and said with a wink, "I should note Will's in the blue shirt so I don't accidentally try to get a good-night kiss from your husband. I never saw two faces that looked more alike."

Elle gave her a demure smile. "I'll make sure you don't get the wrong man."

"Oh, Elle," Mia said with an annoying cackle, "you're so bourgeois."

Will grimaced. *Bourgeois?*

Mia turned her attention to him. "How did you get to be the big cheese at Lambert's Furniture?" Mia reached out and gave his forearm a strong squeeze. "Wow," she said, raising a brow. "Do you work out?"

Will moved his arm and cleared his throat. "Bobby and our cousin Ethan carry a large part of the load. I merely oversee the big picture."

"Oh, modest." Mia looked at Elle. "Don't you just love a strong, modest man?"

"Yes, I do."

When Mia turned her attention to her appetizer plate, Elle cut a glance at Will and mouthed, "I'm sorry."

Will shook his head as if to say, "It's okay."

During dinner Mia continued to dominate the conversation with grand tales of her trips to Europe and the Orient—and not once, but twice more called Elle "bourgeois."

Will couldn't wait for the evening to end.

Around seven, they ordered coffee and dessert. Elle stood and said, "If you'll excuse me, I'm going to the ladies' room."

"I'll go, too." Mia picked up her purse, smoothing her hand along Will's shoulder as she went past, as if they were an intimate couple.

As soon as the women were out of earshot, Will draped his

arm over the back of his chair and regarded Bobby. "Bourgeois? She called your elegant, socially astute wife *bourgeois.*"

Bobby laughed. "I guess she is a little bit of a fruitcake."

"Cotton candy," Will said, his jaw set.

"Cotton candy?" Bobby crinkled his brow.

"Whipped sugar on a stick. All fluff and no substance. An evening with Mia is like consuming *verbal* cotton candy." Will made an *ick* face.

Bobby grinned. "She is beautiful, though. And well traveled."

Will reached for his water. "Look, she's a lovely lady. I don't want to be rude, but she's not for me."

"Maybe she's nervous, Will. Do the Giuseppe's thing, or take her to Sam's Diner. Just the two of you."

"No." Will shook his head and leaned to the side as the waiter placed cheesecake in front of him. "I can tell you now she's not for me. I don't want to waste her time or mine."

Bobby challenged, "You're that sure after one dinner."

"Yes."

Bobby reached for his coffee. "It's your life. I hope you like being a bachelor."

"Bob, I don't want to date just because I'm single."

His brother's perplexed expression made Will laugh.

"Look, I am at peace about being single. I'm content. I'll date when I meet the right one."

Bobby nodded, slicing off a corner of his dessert. "Fine, but I don't think one date is enough. Look at how many people start out hating each other and end up happily married."

"Trust me on this one, I—" A subtle motion across the room caught Will in midsentence. He dropped his linen napkin on the table and stood slowly. Across the room, the Italian Hills' maître d' escorted Grant and Trixie Hanson to a table nearby, and. . .

He couldn't believe it.

"I'm sorry I got you into this," Bobby said.

"Taylor," he said, his gaze following the lithe, exquisite brunette.

two

The maître d' held Taylor's chair as she slid up to the table. "You really didn't have to do this," she said to her parents.

"It's nothing, kiddo. We've been planning to come here for several weeks now." Grant unrolled his silverware from his napkin.

Taylor smiled. "This would be nicer for you and Mom if you didn't have your daughter tagging along." She tapped her chest for emphasis.

"Nonsense," her mother said.

As she reached for her menu, Taylor surveyed the room, the chandelier-and-crystal atmosphere familiar to her. The last time she was here? She thought for a moment. Bobby and Elle's wedding reception. The night she and Will went wading. . .

Taylor shook away the image. *Too long ago to matter now.*

But it was the devastation of that night that made her flee White Birch for New York. In some ways she owed her career to heartbreak and Will Adams.

Her shoulders slumped. Her career. What career? She'd ended that two days ago. No thanks to Lisa Downey. She grabbed her water goblet and took a long drink.

Dad ordered a spinach and artichoke dip with focaccia bread, then turned to Taylor. "What's the plan?"

She put down her menu. "Excuse me?" Was it the lighting, or were her dad's cheeks pale?

"What's the plan? New job? Stay here in White Birch?"

Taylor laughed, reaching for her freshly poured iced tea. "Stay in White Birch? And do what?"

"Get married, give your mom and me more grandkids. Tim's children are practically grown."

"We're ten years apart, Dad." Taylor laughed.

Dad continued, "Claire's eighteen and already graduated. Jarred is sixteen and waiting tables at Sam's, and Quentin is fourteen going on thirty."

Taylor nodded. "He is a little precocious."

"He's very intelligent," Mom added in her best grandma voice.

"Much like you, Taylor. Another whiz kid in the making."

Taylor stared past her father, twisting her napkin with her fingers. "I don't feel like much of a whiz kid."

"Doesn't matter what you feel; it's what you know to be true."

Taylor focused her gaze on her father and smiled. He looked so frail. "Thank you, Dad. And yes," she said as she squared her shoulders, "I'm getting a new job. A better job."

"Taylor, don't you want to marry and have children? You're thirty-three."

"I'm aware of my age, Mom, but I can't leave my career and reputation flapping in the October breeze. I have to reestablish myself or my career is over."

"Seems you've been all about your career for the last decade. Time for real life."

"She'll get there, Trixie. She'll get there. But she's right. She's worked hard. You don't become a principal CPA overnight. Quitting Blankenship and Burns shouldn't be the last line on her résumé."

The waiter brought the bread and sauce appetizer. Grant said a prayer, and Taylor mused over his wisdom. He'd never lived anywhere but White Birch; he'd never worked anywhere but Lambert's Furniture. Sixty-six years in one town, fifty years with one company.

Her parents amazed her.

The waiter came for their dinner order. Taylor ordered the baked ziti with a side salad. Her father ordered lasagna, and her mom ordered the chicken Alfredo.

"I'm splurging tonight." Mom smiled as she folded her menu.

Taylor smiled. "Good for you—" A sudden clatter interrupted

Taylor. She looked across the table to see Dad mopping up his spilled water.

"Dad, are you okay?" Taylor picked up her napkin to help clean the mess, noticing again the pallor of his face.

"I'm all right. Just a little weak from hunger, I guess," Grant said.

"He's fine." Trixie gently pressed the back of her hand against his cheek. "He's fine. Just needs a good meal."

Taylor studied her father for a moment. He didn't look fine, and his wan complexion didn't come from hunger. "Dad, have you been to the doctor?"

"Not yet, no." He kept his gaze on the menu.

Taylor turned to her mom. "Get him to a doctor."

"He's fine, Taylor. He's fine."

"Dad, has this happened before?"

Grant held up his hand. "Taylor, I'll make an appointment."

"Okay."

❧

Will paid the check, and while Bobby helped the ladies with their coats, he whispered to his brother, "I'm going to say hello to Taylor."

Bobby shifted his gaze to the Hansons' table. "Don't make a big deal. You may not want to marry Mia, but she's your date for tonight."

Will held out his hands. "I'm going to say hello to an old friend."

"Then we'll come with you. Elle, Mia, let's go over and say hello to the Hansons."

"Who?" Mia asked, louder than Will thought necessary.

"Some friends of ours," Elle said, smiling, buttoning her top coat button. "Taylor was my maid of honor."

The small blond smiled. "Really." She slipped her arm possessively around Will's.

He winced. If he moved his arm, it would be rude to Mia. But the last thing he wanted clinging to him when he greeted Taylor for the first time in ten years was another woman.

"Good evening, Grant, Trixie," Bobby said, shaking Grant's hand as the man stood. "Hello, Taylor."

"Elle! Bobby. Hello." Taylor rose from her chair.

Will stood back, watching. Her movements were sublime and controlled. He saw a confidence in her words and manner that must have come from living and working in New York.

"Where's her husband?" Mia asked, squeezing his arm.

Will looked down at her. "She's not married."

"Oh," Mia said sharply.

"You have to come over and see our youngest, Max. He's four already," Elle said to Taylor.

"Already? And I've never met him."

Will noticed her fingers tapping against the tabletop.

"Taylor's at the house; give her a call, Elle," Grant said, waving his cheese-covered bread in the air.

"Dad, please." Taylor faked a chuckle. "They don't want to know all about me."

Will recognized the look on her face. Apparently, New York hadn't removed all of her anxieties.

"Of course we do, Taylor. You've got to come over before going back to New York. Please."

"Well, all right." Taylor pressed her hand against the back of her neck, then glanced around at Will.

He waved and moved away from Mia's grip toward Taylor. "Good to see you."

"You're looking well," Taylor said, giving him a slight hug. The clean, subtle scent of her perfume lingered around him. Their eyes met for one brief moment.

"You look amazing," he said.

"Ahem." The blond dynamo sidled up next to Will.

He stepped aside. "Taylor Hanson, I'd like you to meet Mia Wilmington."

"Nice to meet you." Taylor offered her hand.

"Likewise." Mia slipped her arm through Will's.

Will smiled to cover his uneasiness. "Mia teaches at the high school."

Taylor grinned, revealing perfect, white teeth. Will thought she was beautiful. "Very nice." She shifted her gaze toward him.

He knew that look, too. Her "Adams, what are you doing?" look.

Grant brought up the topic of Lambert's Furniture, which took Will and Bobby off in conversation. Elle and Trixie were engaged in a discussion about the last ladies' Bible study, and Mia studied Taylor, arms folded.

Will kept one ear in the conversation with Grant, one listening to Mia and Taylor.

"What do you do?" Mia asked, her voice too sweet.

"I'm a principal CPA," Taylor said with control and grace.

When the waiter appeared with their salads, Will said, "Bobby, we'd better go." He smiled at Taylor. "Good to see you."

She tipped her head. "You, too. Nice to meet you, Mia."

Elle reached for a final hug. "It's been too long."

"I know," Taylor said.

Will was the last one through the door. Glancing over his shoulder, his eyes met hers as she watched him leave.

❧

Late Wednesday afternoon Taylor zipped her overnight bag shut and set it by the bedroom door. She slid a few extra résumés inside her leather portfolio. Tomorrow afternoon she would fly to Charlotte, North Carolina, for her first post–Blankenship & Burns interview.

It had been a week since she left the prestigious New York firm and the life she had built in New York. Mechanically, Taylor moved through the days, one goal in mind: Find a new job.

When Conrad & Associates called Monday morning, her hopes soared.

It had been a long time since she'd interviewed, so as Taylor changed from jeans to running sweats, she mentally rehearsed answers to possible questions.

Conrad: Where do you see yourself in five years?

Taylor: Contributing to the overall vision and goal of Conrad and Associates. Moving toward becoming a partner.

Conrad: What are your greatest strengths?

Taylor: Vision, determination, decisiveness, and ability to focus. Follow-through.

Conrad: Weaknesses?

Taylor: Don't know when to quit, sometimes. Stubborn.

She tied on her running shoes, laughing at herself. Perhaps she'd learned a lesson from the Blankenship experience after all. She was stubborn. More than she knew.

Conrad: How can our firm benefit from hiring you?

Taylor: I have more than ten years' experience in finance, accounting, and investments. I worked at one of the world's most popular financial magazines, Millennium. I'm smart, quick, and an excellent team leader or player, whichever is needed.

Taylor left her room and jogged down the back staircase into the kitchen.

Conrad: Tell us why you left Blankenship & Burns.

"Are you going for a run?" Trixie looked up from where she peeled potatoes, her housedress covered with a wide apron. "Dinner will be ready in an hour."

"Yes." Stretching her legs, Taylor regarded her mom. Trixie Hanson was more like a fifties housewife than a twenty-first-century woman.

Outside, Taylor scanned the orange and red horizon, colored by the setting sun. She drew a deep breath. Cold air, scented with the fragrance of fall leaves, filled her lungs.

Running down Main Street, she kept an even gait, gradually hitting a rhythm, and the anxiety over her life eased.

She would never admit it out loud, but being home—being in White Birch—was like coming home to her best friend. It rejuvenated her, made her focus and remember what's important in life. Odd to think that a town could be her friend. But in many ways, White Birch was just that.

With each step, Taylor reviewed the last few years. Rapid promotions—adding ten or more hours to each workweek. Almost engaged to Ryan Logan. She thanked the Lord many times for saving her from that relationship.

It had been two years since her last vacation. She and her girlfriend, Reneé, had spent a week in Paris. *Ugh, that was exhausting.* Reneé had refused to sleep. She had to see everything; the sunrise, the sunset, the Louvre, every mile along the Seine River. . .

She made a mental note to call Reneé with an update. When Taylor had decided to leave New York, she called the movers, then Reneé.

"Why are you leaving the city? Leave the firm, but stay here," Reneé had insisted with a girlfriend's whine.

"Girl, you know I love you, but it's time for me to move on. Crazy as it seems, quitting has freed me. Now I can see what the rest of the world has to offer."

The feeling of freedom and confidence lasted until Taylor ended the conversation with Reneé and drove out of the city limits. She had battled with anxiety ever since.

But her God was a God of peace. She had to trust in that.

Taylor let her thoughts wander over the past week—dinner with her parents at Italian Hills, her father's pale complexion, Pastor Marlow's Sunday sermon, seeing Bobby and Elle, and Will. . .

Will Adams. Handsome as ever, strong and quiet, speaking volumes with his blue eyes and rakish smile. . .

Taylor wondered about Mia. Though very beautiful, she didn't seem like Will's type. But what did she know after all these years?

Mia certainly seemed into him. Taylor remembered the woman's possessive hook on Will's arm.

As she headed down Main Street and rounded the corner toward Milo Park, she heard the echo of a bouncing ball then the rattle of a hoop.

She slowed her pace as she neared the courts, stopping to peer through the chain-link fence.

Catching her breath, she couldn't help but grin and challenge the lone player. "You still any good at one-on-one?"

three

Will turned at the sound of her voice. In a million years, he couldn't have suppressed his smile.

He dribbled in place, regarding Taylor from midcourt. "I'm still better than you, if that's what you mean."

"You think so?" She rounded the fence, tall and angular in her baggy red sweats and faded university sweatshirt. It hung loose about her torso, and the ends of her short, chestnut-brown hair pointed in all directions.

Will laughed. "Any day of the week and twice on Sunday." Harry bounded across the court, his tongue dangling from the side of his mouth.

"And who is this?"

"Harry."

Taylor leaned forward and met him nose to nose. Harry surprised her with a sloppy kiss.

She wiped her nose with the edge of her sleeve and winked up at Will. "Harry, please. We just met." Harry nudged her again, and she buried her face in the fur around his neck. "He's beautiful."

Will watched with a grin. "He's an Old English sheepdog rescue. Some family in Maine couldn't care for him, so I adopted him a couple of years ago."

Taylor looked up. "He's a lucky dog."

"I believe you challenged me to a game of one-on-one."

She stood straight, her hands on her hips. "I believe I did."

Will motioned to the side of the court. "Harry, go lie down."

The big dog hesitated, looking between Taylor and Will as if he wasn't sure whether he wanted to obey his master or stay with his new friend. "Harry, lie down," Will repeated, pointing courtside.

This time, Harry obediently loped over to the grass.

Will tucked the ball under his arm. "Look at you. One face lick and you've captured the affection of my dog."

"Seems to be my only talent these days."

Will raised a brow, wondering what that was supposed to mean, but let the comment go. He bounce-passed the ball to her. "Ladies first."

"I haven't played in a while," Taylor said, dribbling, squaring off in front of Will.

"Whoa now, no excuses. You challenged me, remember?"

She laughed, and he remembered how much he loved the melody of her merriment.

With a mischievous glint in her eyes, she taunted him. "Is that a spare tire around your middle, Adams, or have you put on a few pounds?"

Will guffawed and patted his belly. "Nothing spare around here, Hanson. You worry about yourself. Having worked a desk job and all, I'm wondering if you have the stamina for this."

On the heels of his last word, Taylor drove the ball up the middle of the lane. Will moved into her path, but she shoved past him for an easy layup.

"I believe that's one for me and nothing for you." She tossed him the ball then turned in a circle, waving her index fingers in the air. "One to nothing, one to nothing."

Will shook his head, bouncing the ball. "You are so going to be humiliated, Hanson."

She made a funny face. "We'll see."

He'd forgotten how competitive she was. "First player to twenty-one wins," he said.

"What's the prize?" Taylor asked, leaning forward, her hands on her knees.

The word came without thought but from the depths of his heart. "Dinner."

Taylor stood upright, her jaw jutted forward. Will thought he saw a flicker of. . .what? Anger? Doubt? Resistance?

After a second, she said, "What about your girlfriend, Mia?"

Will squared his shoulders. "She's not my girlfriend. Just a dinner date."

"Does she know that?"

"I made no promises, if that's what you mean." Will bounced the ball once.

"All right, then, dinner," Taylor said.

Will smiled with a nod, then jumped into motion, running around the top of the basketball key. "Good. I hear your New York salary can afford to take me to a nice place."

Taylor tried to block, but he ran around her for an outside jump shot. An easy point.

Taylor took the ball, recounting the score. "One to one."

"Getting scared yet?"

"No, are you?" she asked with a sideways smirk.

Actually, yes—afraid of falling in love before the game is over.

Taylor made another basket, then he made two as daylight faded to dusk. Will played hard, but as always, Taylor proved to be a worthy competitor.

When the score reached fifteen to sixteen, Will called for a time-out. "I need a little water."

Taylor smiled. "I just ran five miles, and you don't see me begging for water."

"Overachiever."

"Jealous."

To Will, the whole scenario was like a picture out of their past. After high school, most of their friends married or moved away from White Birch, so Will and Taylor spent nearly every college summer break together, shooting hoops, taking long runs, or grabbing pizza at Giuseppe's. Then, during Bobby and Elle's wedding festivities, their relationship had spiked to a new level.

"Let's go." Taylor clapped her hands, the sound reverberating in the cold air.

Will took a last sip from the water fountain and dribbled the ball back to the court. He made an easy shot before Taylor was in place.

"Cheater," she protested with a laugh then took the ball and shot over Will's head.

"Sixteen to seventeen."

Will watched her, bemused. "Still think you can win?"

"Just make your shot, Adams. Stop stalling."

When the score tied at twenty, Will had the ball. "This is it. No backing out now. You're buying me dinner."

"Unless you lose." Taylor bounced side to side on the balls of her feet. Will chuckled at her energy. Sweaty and red-faced, yes, but she looked incredible anyway.

He drove up the lane, then stopped. Taylor rushed him, arms up, going for the block. Will aimed at the basket and released the ball right over her head.

Swish. The ball sank through the net.

Taylor flew past him, moaning as he scored the winning point. He retrieved the ball, tucked it under his arm, and slapped Taylor with a high five.

"Nice win, Will." She ran her hand through her hair, making it stand even more on end.

"Hey," he said softly, "you don't really owe me dinner."

"A deal's a deal."

Will walked over to the side of the court where his jacket lay. "Tell you what, dinner at my place. You bring the trimmings; I'll provide a couple of steaks."

Taylor hesitated. "I was thinking more like Giuseppe's."

"All right. Tomorrow?"

"I can't." She offered no more information.

"Friday night?"

She nodded. "Friday night. Six?"

He agreed, motioning for her to walk with him to his truck. "Harry, let's go, boy." Will whistled and the dog came running.

Taylor stopped short and squinted at her watch. "Dinner." She tapped the face of her timepiece. "Mom said it'd be ready in an hour." She looked up at Will. "I've been gone almost two hours." She turned to run home.

"Taylor, Taylor! My truck's right here." Will ran after her

and grabbed her by the arm. "I'll give you a ride."

He opened the passenger door for her then climbed in behind the wheel. Thirty seconds later, they were cruising down Main Street toward the Hanson home.

He cleared his throat and glanced sideways at her, trying to think of something to say that wasn't sports related.

In the soft light of the dashboard, he could see the glow on her face from exercise and the cold.

How is it that it felt so right to be with her? After so many years. . . It astounded him.

"How long is the whiz kid in town?" he ventured in a casual tone.

She smiled but looked away, out the window. "Not long."

Will nodded once. With the energy of basketball fading, Taylor's bright countenance seemed to fade. "Does your dad still call you the whiz kid?"

She nodded, looking over at him. "He does."

"The whiz kid," Will repeated.

"Anyone good at computers, math, or numbers is a whiz kid to him."

"Oh, no, but you're not just good at computers and math. You're the volleyball star, basketball MVP, debate team captain— I think you even won a spelling bee or two."

"Okay, okay." She held up her hand for him to stop.

"The whiz kid," he whispered with a light laugh.

She gave him a smirk. "And who, driving this truck, was Mr. Football and the baseball home run king? Hmm? I believe he also got *all A*s, *all* four years of high school."

Will laughed. "Touché. I had a few Bs. Maybe."

Taylor said, "Right," with a snort. "Now you're Mr. President."

"How'd you know about me taking over Lambert's Furniture?"

"Dad. Who else?" She picked at the fuzz balls on her sweatpants. "Do you like it?"

He grinned. "I do. Bobby oversees sales. Ethan is over production."

"Guess you got what you wanted."

He sensed her gazing at him. "I guess so."

"You told me you wanted to run the family business the night of Bobby and Elle's wedding, remember?"

He remembered. The night he let her go. "When we were at the covered bridge."

"Yes."

Will slowed the truck as he turned into the Hansons' driveway. Taylor opened her door before he came to a complete stop.

"Thanks." She hopped out.

"Taylor, I—"

Taylor looked back at him. "I know, Will. Look, it's been a long time. Forgotten, forgiven. . .a distant memory."

"I'm sorry for the way it ended."

"Yeah, me, too." She shoved the door shut and disappeared in the darkness.

&.

As the jet taxied off the runway in Charlotte, Taylor settled in her seat, breathing a sigh of relief. She'd had an exceptional day. She loved the staff of Conrad & Associates. They were talented, enthusiastic, and reaching for the stars.

Taylor's interview with her potential boss, Katie Myers, Conrad's partner over investments and accounting, went exceptionally well.

Leaning her head against the side of the plane, she peered out the window. "Lord, this felt so right."

But was it right? Taylor drew a deep breath, twisted in her seat, and fought off a pang of anxiety. She needed this job. She needed to get her career back on track or fall by the wayside. Taylor exhaled, trying not to obsess.

As she tipped her head back against her seat, she thought of home. Her mother's cooking, her father's colorful tales from the workday, her brother Tim and his wife, Dana. . . Their children Claire, Jarred, and Quentin. . .

She'd missed a lot of family time over the years while chasing a corporate CPA career. She'd also missed a lot of time talking to Jesus. How easily the issues of life, busyness, and work overshadowed her desire to know Him more.

Suddenly, an image of Will bounced into her thoughts. She grinned, eyes still closed, remembering their basketball game. *That was fun.*

Jerky, faded images from her past rolled across her mind like an old-time picture show. A collage of all her times with Will, one scene playing after another until she wondered if she'd ever had a life without him.

She opened her eyes with a start and sat forward, shaking the images loose, pressing the palm of her hand against her forehead.

four

On Friday morning Will sat with Bobby and Ethan in the main conference room with their laptops and the third quarter financial reports, discussing plans for next year's revenue.

Ethan sighed and slumped down in his chair. "I don't know. What's the initial investment, Will? For the new business system?"

"Eth, we've got to do this. Invest money to earn money," Bobby said, getting up for a cold soda. "Streamline our inventory and accounting."

"Would you grab me one, too?" Will said, holding out his hand. Across from him, Ethan stared at the ceiling. "What's your hesitation, Ethan?"

Ethan motioned to all the data on the table. "I convinced you guys to spend thousands of dollars to retool half the shop last year, and we still haven't gotten a return on that investment." He flicked at one of the reports. "At least not according to these records."

Bobby handed Will a cold soda. "The summer was slower than usual. But, Ethan, we've got to grow the business office or we can't launch our e-business. When I met with Web Warehouse last week to approve the new site they are designing, I was convinced we made the right decision to create a web store."

Ethan shook his head. "I know, I know. But installing a new business system will take a ton of time. We'll have to train the financial staff and all the supervisors and team leads."

Will popped the soda top and stood. "We've got enough in the capital budget for overtime and training." Will looked at Bobby, then Ethan. "We have to do this."

"Will, we make furniture. Beautiful, fine furniture," Ethan

said. "We know nothing about installing a new accounting system. It will overload Markie."

Will grinned. "Markie wants this more than I do. She tells me every day we're holding the accounting system together with twine."

Ethan moaned. "You're right."

"She's a good financial manager. If she says we need a new system, we need a new system."

Bobby agreed. "You're right. Let's do it."

Ethan sat forward, gathered his reports, and powered down his laptop. "We have the new warehouse only half to capacity. It wouldn't hurt to get the e-business running full steam."

Will nodded. "Now you're thinking like a CEO, Eth."

Ethan stuffed his bag with the production reports and his computer. "Yeah, that's what I was going for, Will." He laughed. "I'll see you. I've got a to-do list a mile long, and Julie and I are meeting her folks for dinner."

Bobby picked up his laptop. "Will, I'll call Hayes Business Systems and tell them we're ready to deal."

"Thanks, Bobby. I'll get with Markie and look over the schedule to see when would be the best time to do an installation." Will sat down, feeling the weight of the company's success on his shoulders for the first time in a long time. He sighed.

Bobby stopped in the doorway. "When we took over this company, we promised ourselves we'd be innovative and take risks."

"I know, and we're keeping that promise."

Will was deep in thought when the emergency buzzer resounded from the manufacturing floor. He jumped from his chair and ran into his office, Bobby coming in right behind. Together, they peered through the long production window.

Several workers huddled around a fallen man. Grant. Will stormed out and down the metal stairs to where Grant lay on the cold production floor.

Will shoved his way into the huddle where a crew member

checked the vitals on an unconscious, pallid Grant.

"He just collapsed," someone said.

"We called 9-1-1," added another.

When the paramedics arrived, they took over. The flurry of activity never stopped, and as the paramedics loaded Grant into the ambulance, an oxygen mask on his face, Will snatched up his cell phone and dialed the Hansons'. "Trixie, it's Will Adams." He tried to sound cheerful, but his voice choked as the sirens wailed.

"Will?" Trixie's voice quivered.

"Grant collapsed."

ฆ

"He has to be all right. He has to be."

"Mom, he will be." Taylor guided her distraught mother through the ER doors where Will waited for them.

"Will, how is he?" Trixie pressed her hand on his arm.

"Better. I'll take you to him." Will glanced over his shoulder at Taylor. "The doctor said just one visitor at a time until he goes up to his room."

"Of course." Taylor watched her frightened mother disappear down the hall, Will's arm around her shoulders. *God, not Daddy. Don't take him home now.*

She sat in a worn waiting room chair, flipping absently through a celebrity magazine, feeling as if everything in her life teetered on the brink of disaster.

She tossed the magazine aside and looked up as Will walked toward her. He exuded such a confidence and peace; his presence was like a cool glass of water at the end of a long, hot day. When life buzzed with confusion, Will brought clarity.

"Your dad was glad to see your mom," Will said, his blue eyes steady on her as he sat in the adjacent chair.

She smiled though her bottom lip trembled. "How is he?"

"He's going to be fine, Taylor." Will pressed his hand on her back.

"He looked so pale at dinner the other night." Taylor covered her face with her hands. She didn't want to cry. She wanted to be strong for Mom.

"Hey, hey." Will cradled her head on his shoulder, stroking her hair. "Let's go sit someplace quiet."

Taylor followed him to the chapel, enjoying the sensation of being led. She spent so much of her time the last ten years out front, directing, leading.

The interior of the chapel was peaceful, but cool. Taylor shivered, rubbing her hands along her arms.

"We left in such a hurry I forgot my jacket."

"Guess they don't turn the heat up in here." Will shrugged out of his coat and draped it over Taylor's shoulders.

"Now you'll be cold," Taylor said, settling in the last of the red-cushioned pews.

"Don't worry about me." He sat in the pew in front of hers, angled sideways to see her.

Taylor regarded him for a moment. She loved the symmetry of his face. It was as if the Lord took extra care in aligning his features. And his skin. . . Most of her girlfriends paid top dollar for something he probably took for granted and washed with deodorant soap.

"What?" Will asked.

Taylor glanced away. "What?"

"You were staring at me."

Taylor bit her lower lip, her gaze downcast. "Now why would I stare at you, Will Adams?"

He chuckled. "You tell me. Do I have something on my face, in my teeth? Is my hair sticking up?"

Taylor smiled. "No, no. If you must know, I was thinking what great skin you have. It's downright wrong for a man to have such small pores."

Will laughed. "You're very strange, Taylor."

"I know, but that's why you love me." Taylor meant for the words to sound light and airy, like a joke, but they came with an echo from a deep, hidden place in her soul. She squirmed.

"I suppose you're right," Will said, his words weighty and real, as if emerging from a dark corridor of time.

When their eyes met, he coughed and twisted around. Taylor's heart thumped in her chest.

They sat in silence for the next few minutes. Taylor wondered what he was thinking but didn't want to ask. Not now, not here.

He got up and walked toward the front of the chapel. She could see his lips moving in prayer.

Taylor wanted to pray, but inner turmoil stifled her words.

"Did you call your brother?" Will asked as he turned to her.

Taylor made a face. "No, I completely forgot." She dug her cell phone from her purse and stepped into the hallway.

Outside the door, she paused for a moment, trembling. She inhaled a cleansing breath. *It's been ten years, Will. Ten years and you still get to me. Still.*

With a press of a few buttons, she dialed her brother. "Tim, Dad's in the hospital."

a

Will watched Taylor through the narrow window in the chapel door. What was he thinking? He'd practically told her he loved her.

Did he love her? And what about her comment "that's why you love me"? Did she love him? They barely knew each other anymore.

Will paced up the chapel aisle, wondering how long she'd be in town. If she hung around too long, he felt confident he'd fall in love with her—if he'd ever stopped loving her in the first place.

"Tim's on his way," Taylor said when she reentered the chapel, dropping her cell phone in her bag.

Will nodded. "Good." He recognized her purse as a famous designer bag. Elle had bought one a few years ago. He remembered his brother and sister-in-law had waged war over the price of that bag for two days.

He guessed Taylor's New York City CPA salary afforded her those kinds of amenities.

Will grinned. She looked good in his jacket. Absently, he

reached up and straightened the collar. "We were supposed to have pizza tonight."

Her eyes widened. "You're right." She motioned over her shoulder. "I hear the food here is terrible, but I'm buying if you're game."

Will made a face. "Are you kidding me? Our deal was for Giuseppe's. I'm not cashing in for hospital grub."

Taylor shrugged playfully. "Fine, then you can buy."

"Fine." Will bumped her as they walked toward the door, shoulder to shoulder.

She smiled at him, grabbed her purse from the pew, and bumped him back.

In the cafeteria, they ordered burgers and fries and large diet sodas.

Will bit into his hamburger. "Hmm. I thought you said the food here was terrible."

Taylor shook her head. "No, I said I *heard* the food was terrible."

He laughed. "Well, now we know you *heard* wrong."

"Yum, you could bring me on a date here." She glanced up quickly, as if catching her words.

"I will."

"I mean in general—*you*—as in. . ." She motioned with her hand, sitting with her back stiff. "People in general, could, um. . ." She coughed.

"Exit, stage left."

Her shoulders collapsed. "I think I will." She sipped her soda. "So, did you ever get your MBA?"

Will swallowed and wiped his mouth with his napkin, his heart thumping a little harder. Another pointer back to that night on the bridge. "Yes."

Taylor nodded, pulling the tomato from her burger. "Good for you. What else have you been doing besides taking over the family business?"

"I ran for town council. Beat old Walter Burnett out of his seat."

She grinned. "In general, ruling the world."

"Keeps me out of trouble." Will smiled. "What about Taylor Jo Hanson? How many worlds have you conquered?"

A sadness flicked across her eyes, and she concentrated too long on squirting ketchup over her fries. "Not many."

He coughed. "I find that hard to believe."

She jutted out her chin. "I quit." The words came out like a one-two punch. *I quit.*

He glanced up, confused. "Quit what?" He furrowed his brow.

"I quit my job."

"Really?" Will watched and waited, wondering if she would explain, but she didn't. "That doesn't sound like you. Quitting."

Taylor squared her shoulders. "No, but sometimes a girl has to do what a girl has to do."

"You're looking for a new job then?"

"I had an interview with a CPA firm in Charlotte a few days ago." She wiped her hands with her napkin. "It went really well."

The familiar "oh" of disappointment pinged in Will's heart. "Charlotte's a great city."

"Yes, I know." But Will knew in that instant he didn't want her to leave White Birch. He didn't have to think about it or ponder why. He just knew. "Taylor, do you think you might—"

"Taylor!" Tim Hanson rushed into the cafeteria. "I've been looking for you; we can see Dad now. Hi, Will."

Will shook his hand. "Tim."

Taylor stood, reaching for her handbag and slipping out of Will's coat. "Thanks for the burger." She smiled. "And the coat."

"Anytime." He watched her walk away, the words he wanted to say stuck in his throat, making it hard to breathe.

five

Monday morning Taylor's cell phone woke her from a fitful sleep. Distorted dreams plagued her during the night, and she felt more tired now than she had before she went to bed.

Shouldn't have had that last cup of coffee.

She stumbled out of bed and padded across her room to her dresser where her phone sat, hooked to the charger. "Hello."

"Taylor Hanson, please."

"Speaking." Taylor rubbed her eyes with her fingers, squinting as a flood of morning light streamed through the opened blinds.

"Good morning. This is Gina Abernathy from Conrad & Associates."

Taylor's eyes popped open. "Good morning." She smoothed her hand on her pajama pants and looked out the window. It was a beautiful fall morning.

"You impressed our team, and we enjoyed meeting you."

"Thank you. Conrad is an excellent organization." The windowpane reflected Taylor's smile.

"We've filled the position you interviewed for, but we'll keep your résumé on file."

"I see." Taylor knew the routine from here. Thanks but no thanks. She'd done it to dozens of potential candidates at Blankenship & Burns.

She thanked Gina Abernathy, pressed END, and set the phone down. Shoving the window open, she welcomed the cold breeze against her face, cooling the heat of disappointment.

She thought she had that job. "Lord, now what?"

"Taylor?" Mom appeared in the doorway, her robe belted around her small frame. She looked tired. "You'll catch your death with that window open. Shut it. I can't have you collapsing on me, too."

33

"Sorry." She tugged on the window's frame. "The company in Charlotte called."

Mom clasped her hands together and sat on the edge of the bed. "Well, I suppose you'll be leaving soon, then."

"I didn't get the job." Taylor fell against the windowsill.

Mom straightened the edge of her robe. "The Lord has something better for you, angel."

Taylor sloughed over to the bed and fell back on her pillow. "I'm sure He does; I just wish I knew what." She hated being suspended between her past and her future.

Mom patted Taylor's leg. "He'll let you know."

"I have to believe He will; otherwise my stomach will stay knotted for the rest of my life."

"I'm going to the hospital to make your Dad's 10:00 a.m. doctor's appointment. He's going to recommend a procedure."

"I'll come later. I want to stay here. Pray. Call a few people. Look for leads." She hadn't done any job searching over the weekend; she'd worried over Dad.

Mom stood. "Taylor, you've always accomplished whatever you wanted. You're our whiz kid."

Some whiz kid. Besides, she hadn't gotten *everything* in life she wanted. Will came to mind. "Thank you, Mom. Kiss Dad for me."

As her mom exited, Taylor closed her bedroom door, grabbed her Bible, and curled up on her bed with her fretful thoughts.

"Okay, Lord, I surrender it all to You. The Bible says, 'be anxious for nothing,' but I need a job—the right job."

She thought of Will's strong and peaceful countenance. "And I need peace, Lord."

ye

Will looked over his shoulder when a knock echoed outside his door. He smiled. "Grandpa, come in."

Somberly, the Lambert patriarch entered, his hands in his jacket pockets. "Just came from seeing Grant."

Harry trotted over to Grandpa, his tail wagging.

"I e-mailed the staff this morning to let them know what's going on."

Grandpa jutted out his chin and began petting Harry's head, absently. "The doctor is recommending angioplasty."

Will leaned back in his chair. "Angioplasty is less intrusive than open-heart surgery."

"Trixie's relieved about it. She came in this morning with her hair and makeup done, wearing a suit with matching shoes and hat, all smiles for Grant."

"I wouldn't expect anything less from her."

"She's a rock on the outside, but I'm afraid she's putty on the inside. Your grandma took her for coffee to make sure she's doing well."

"I grabbed a bite with Taylor Friday night at the hospital. She seemed to be taking it well."

Grandpa raised a brow. "Ole Taylor—"

Will sat forward. "Don't get any ideas."

"Me?" Grandpa pointed to himself. "I'm already married. You are the one who needs to be getting some ideas."

"Not so sure Taylor wants me having ideas about her."

"Aha, is she the one?"

"The one what?"

Grandpa chuckled. "The one you've been waiting for all this time."

Will focused on his computer. "Don't you have someplace to go?" he asked, glancing back at his grandfather.

Grandpa rubbed his chin then said, "No, I've got all morning to hang around here."

Will waved toward the door. "Then go bug Ethan or something."

His grandfather chuckled again.

"What about me?" Ethan walked into the office and plopped into the chair across from Will's desk. Harry left Grandpa and plopped his chin on Ethan's knee.

Grandpa spoke first. "We were just talking about—"

"Nothing." Will eyed Grandpa.

"Good," Ethan said, scratching Harry behind the ears. "We need to talk about Grant's replacement until he's back on his feet."

"Hire me."

Will and Ethan stared at their grandfather.

"I'm available and could fill in for a few weeks. I did start this company, after all. I know most of the crew and the procedures."

Ethan looked at Will. "He's got a point."

Will regarded his grandfather. "I don't know."

Ethan stood. Harry retreated to his corner and curled up on his bed. "He's perfect, Will. Grandpa, you're hired."

Will grinned. "Fine." He pointed at the older Lambert. "But don't be bugging me about. . .stuff."

"Taylor?" Grandpa asked.

"What's this?" Ethan prodded, leaning on the edge of Will's desk.

"Taylor's back in town," Grandpa said.

"I know. Julie said she saw her the other night at Italian Hills. Will, is there something starting up again with—"

Will leapt to his feet. "Stop." He looked at Ethan. "Taylor quit her job in New York. But she interviewed in Charlotte and will probably be moving there soon."

"She didn't get the job," Grandpa said like a seasoned anchorman.

Will stared at him, his hands on his hips. "How do you know?"

Grandpa walked toward the door and motioned to Ethan. "Better show me around the production floor, refresh my memory."

Will shook his head as he watched them leave. Grandpa stepped back and stuck his head in the doorway. "Why don't you call her and find out?"

Will sat down, hard. Grandpa had a way of pushing his buttons. All the right ones. For a few minutes he pondered calling Taylor, and just as he reached for the phone, it rang.

"Will Adams."

"Hi, it's Taylor." Her voice reminded him of velvet.

He cleared his throat. "How are you?"

"Fine, all things considered." She chuckled.

"Tough week?"

"Tough couple of weeks."

Will leaned back in his chair. "I'm sorry."

She laughed. "It's not your fault."

"No, I guess not." He loved Taylor's forthrightness.

"Daddy is scheduled for angioplasty tomorrow. He's going down to Manchester tonight."

"Grandpa told me," he said, wondering if she'd tell him about Charlotte.

She sighed. "Dad's in good spirits and other than his arteries, he's in good health."

Will prodded her more. "Everything else going okay?"

"If I said, I might give in and cry."

"A good cry never hurt anyone."

She laughed. "Moving on. . . Thanks for being there Friday for Mom and me."

"Not a problem. Tell your dad Grandpa's filling in for him."

"He was already telling the doctor he needed to be back to work next week."

Will grinned. "Sounds like your pop."

"Yeah, well Trixie the Terrible is on the scene, and Dad won't be back to work until she says so. She's insisting he use up some vacation."

Will laughed. "He has a lot of time banked. Tell him to relax, burn up some vacation, and heal."

"I will."

Then, as suddenly as the conversation started, it ended. Will wanted to ask about her job but hesitated. Too personal. If she wanted him to know about Charlotte, she would tell him.

Then he had an idea. "You still owe me pizza."

"Right, I do."

"You'll be with your dad tonight and tomorrow. So—"

"I'll be home tomorrow night by eight." Her tone sounded promising.

"Say eight thirty? Meet you at Giuseppe's."

"I'd like that."

"See you then."

⁂

Taylor ladled soup into bowls and flipped the grilled cheese sandwiches on the griddle. Mom dropped ice into the glasses on the table with a *clink-clink* and filled them with iced tea.

"Tim, you want one or two sandwiches?" Taylor called.

"Two," Tim answered from the living room, where he was arranging kindling in the fireplace. "Mom, where'd Dad put the matches?"

"Oh, he uses one of those long lighter things. Look in the end table drawer." Trixie motioned in the air with her slender hand.

"Dad looked good tonight," Taylor said, reflecting on their trip to the hospital in Manchester where Grant had been transported. He had a nice private room.

Tim came around the corner. "It's still hard to imagine Dad in that hospital bed."

Mom fluttered around the kitchen, opening and closing doors without retrieving anything. "Well now, he'll be just fine. Just fine."

Taylor handed Tim a plate and a bowl. "Dr. Elliot said the surgeon in Manchester is one of the best." She touched her mother's arm. "Dad will come through with flying colors."

Trixie's lips quivered when she smiled. "He is in good health otherwise, isn't he?"

"Remember that health food kick he went on about twenty-five, thirty years ago?" Tim laughed, biting into his sandwich. A string of melted cheese stuck to his chin.

Taylor passed him a napkin, grinning. "Barely. I was what, six? You were sixteen?"

Trixie smiled. "He was so determined to get this family healthy."

"Were we sick?" Taylor asked.

"Oh, no, but your dad wanted to ensure long, happy lives for all of us."

Still laughing, Tim reminisced, pointing at Taylor. "Remember when old Smokey dug up the bread you buried in the backyard?"

She pounded the table. "Dad was so mad. But I thought the bread was made of twigs or something." She made a face, remembering.

"Oh, it was horrible bread," Trixie said, spooning a bite of soup.

"It made the worst peanut butter and jelly sandwiches," Taylor added.

"And that was the only thing you would eat that year," Tim reminded her.

"I remember."

"Speaking of eating." Tim popped open a bag of baked chips. "That was a cozy scene I walked into the other night with you and Will in the hospital cafeteria."

Taylor choked. "Cozy? A burger in the hospital cafeteria?"

"Maybe your old crush isn't so old."

"Have you gone crazy?"

"Taylor, lower your voice. Ladies don't shout."

She gaped at her mom. "And gentlemen don't make assumptions." She whispered toward Tim. "Have you gone crazy?"

Laughing, Tim scooted away from the table for more soup. "He's a great catch, Tay."

He didn't have to remind her. "I'm not looking for a man; I'm looking for a job, Tim."

"You could stay in White Birch and work for me. Dana's busy hauling Jarred and Quentin all over town. Claire's eighteen and doesn't want to admit she knows us."

"You actually want me to come down there and work in your office? You're an architect, Tim. I know nothing about building buildings."

"You don't fool me, Taylor. I could teach you CAD in a week."

She shook her head. "I'm a CPA, Tim, not a CAD operator."

"Well, I offered."

After Tim left for home and Mom readied for bed, Taylor decided to check her phone and e-mail for any messages. There were two job postings, but they were just above entry level and she wasn't sure she wanted to drop that far down the ladder. So far, Tim's offer was the best thing going.

Taylor shoved her laptop aside and dropped her head on her desk. She hated feeling anxious, but there it was, gripping her middle—gripping her heart and mind.

"Lord, I can't continue like this. I need Your peace. It's been so long."

Almost instantly, she thought of Will. It was his peaceful aura that attracted her to him as much as his blue eyes and broad, white smile.

six

Will waited for Taylor in the back of Giuseppe's. The smell of garlic and baking dough stirred his appetite. He rapped his knuckles against the table in a steady beat, eager to see her. When she walked through the door, he smiled and stood to greet her. *Give her a hug,* he thought. But she stuck out her hand before he got close.

"Hi," she said, slipping her hand into his.

"Hi, back," he said, liking the feel of her palm against his. They slipped into the booth, sitting across from each other.

"Welcome to Giuseppe's." The proprietor's big voice bellowed toward them, all the consonants accented and rolling. "Will, who is this–a pretty lady?"

Will grinned. "You know Taylor Hanson, Giuseppe."

The big man's hands shot to his face and covered his jiggling cheeks. "Taylor, what is wrong? So thin. So thin."

She pinched her lips together, though a smile tugged at the corners of her mouth. "I lost a few pounds. Five years ago."

Giuseppe stuck his finger in the air. "I get extra garlic rolls with extra butter." He hurried away.

Taylor laughed, wrinkling her nose at Will. "Extra butter? That means an *extra* mile for me tomorrow." She unzipped her jacket.

"I love that about Giuseppe. In his eyes, no one can be too. . . endowed." Will reached for her coat and folded it on top of his.

Their waiter, Brandon, stopped by for their drink order, and Will asked Taylor, "Large pizza? The three cheese is excellent."

Her eyes sparkled when she looked at him. Didn't they? Or was he just imagining?

"Sounds good. I'm starved," she said.

Giuseppe swooped in with a large basket of bread and

instructed Brandon to "keep it full."

"You're much-a too skinny, Taylor. Much-a."

"I'll work on it," Taylor promised with a wink.

When Giuseppe was gone, Will prayed over the food and the evening. After he said amen, he handed Taylor a plate with two garlic rolls. "You're not, you know."

She reached for her napkin. "Not what?"

Brandon set their drinks on the table. "Your pizza will be right up."

Will nodded to Brandon then answered Taylor. "Too skinny."

"Are you suggesting I'm overweight?"

Will laughed heartily. "I guess I'm treading on dangerous ground, aren't I?" She grinned and nodded as he sipped his soda and decided to change the subject. "How's your dad?"

"The angioplasty went very well. He looks a hundred percent better already. He's probably coming home tomorrow."

Will nodded. "We prayed for him this morning in our staff meeting."

Taylor tore a bite off her garlic roll. "You guys pray every morning?"

"Yes."

"I could've used prayer at the firm in New York," Taylor said in a soft, thoughtful tone.

"You want to tell me what happened?"

"Not really."

He reached for another roll. "Okay."

"I'd had enough," she said without preamble. "I had an egotistical boss—one of the partners—who drove me crazy. I worked seventy, eighty hours a week, and finally, I'd had enough."

"Good for you."

Taylor slapped her hands against the table. "Good for me? I'm unemployed. I own a brand-new imported car, my furniture is in storage, and a marvelous job opportunity in North Carolina passed me by."

"So what? You have a mountain of experience, and you're

excellent at what you do, whiz kid. The Lord has something for you." Will suddenly had an idea. He'd have to run it by Bobby for a sanity check, but it just might be brilliant.

Taylor lowered her gaze, her slender hands around the small white plate holding her uneaten roll. "You make it sound so easy, so not-a-big-deal."

"I know it is a big deal, but, Taylor, you're so much more than your career. You know, when I want to carve something special, I hunt for the right piece of wood. At first, it's just a block with nice grain and maybe a fragrance like cedar. Then I start cutting, shaping, sanding. . . The wood becomes something beautiful. That's you in God's hands."

She regarded him. "What an amazing image. Thank you." With that, she sat back, dropping her arms to her sides, and stared out the window. "I just am so mad at myself for quitting. There had to be a better solution."

"Sometimes *resigning* is the solution. To act when you know it's time to move on."

"Pizza." Brandon cleared room for a large, round tray with a hot, thin-crust pizza oozing with cheese.

"I wish I had your confidence. . .and peace."

"Well," Will said, shoveling a cheesy slice onto Taylor's plate, "hang around me for a while, and I might let you have some for free."

⁂

On a crisp, cold Sunday afternoon, Taylor donned her sweats and jogged to Milo Park.

Dad was home now, and Mom flitted around the house like a hen with coop full of chicks. Taylor grinned, pressing her hand to her stomach as she remembered the four-course lunch Mom served after church.

As for Taylor, she spent an hour surfing for job openings, submitting her résumé online, and trying to get her foot in the door, any door. Last week it seemed every contact she called was either out of the office or "no longer with us."

When Will had called an hour earlier with a flag football

invitation, she had jumped at the chance to move her cramped muscles.

As she ran toward the field, she could see a dozen or so guys gathering.

Five minutes later, the blue flag and white flag teams were chosen, then Will reviewed the rules. Last, he said, "Taylor, as our only woman player, is wearing orange flags. She's a wide receiver. Anyone grab anything but a flag, you're out of the game." Will jerked his thumb over his shoulder and shot each guy an intense glance. When his gaze fell on Taylor, she nodded her thanks.

"Since there's only eleven of us, we'll play half field. Huddle up."

Jordan West, the star quarterback at White Birch High when Will played running back, led the white flag team. Will quarterbacked the blue flag team.

"Hi, Taylor," Jordan said, tapping her on the arm. "I didn't know you were in town."

She smiled. "Yes, briefly." Jordan looked so much the same. Broad-shouldered and slender. . . Sparkling brown eyes. . . His blond hair was thinner than she remembered, though.

"I heard about your dad. I hope he's doing well."

"He's doing very well, thank you. He's home, and Mom is in her element taking care of him."

೫

"Hanson, let's go," Will bellowed, motioning for her to join the huddle.

"Better go," she said to Jordan, moving backward.

"Talk to you later. After the game maybe."

She nodded. "Maybe."

"What was that all about?" Will whispered when she joined the huddle.

"Nunya," she said with a smirk.

"Nunya?" He furrowed his brow. "What?"

"Nunya business." She laughed and clapped him on the shoulder. "None of your business."

"Har, har," he said. In the huddle, Will instructed his team. "They have one more player than we do, but we have Speedy Gonzales here." He pointed to Taylor. "On two, Cimowsky, you sweep around behind me. I'll fake a handoff." Will pointed to Taylor. "Run up the middle ten yards, turn, and I'll pass it to you."

"Do you want me to count one Mississippi, two Mississippi, three—"

Will bumped her with his hip. "No. I want you to run ten yards, turn, and catch."

She snickered. "Testy."

Will ignored her. "Everyone else, block. On three."

"Break!" The team of five moved to the line of scrimmage.

Taylor lined up on the right, her adrenaline pumping. *This is going to be a blast.* She could already feel the week's subtle frustrations burning away.

Will walked behind her and touched her back. "Go for the touchdown," he said in a low voice.

She nodded. She knew what to do. Jordan lined up across from her. He smiled. She smiled. Will shouted "Two!" and Taylor went into motion.

As Taylor cut up the middle, Jordan backpedaled, calling to his scattered team, "He's passing to Taylor!" *Ten yards, turn, and look at Will.* Her gaze connected with his as he released the ball. It spiraled through the air and into her arms.

She ran for the goal, marked by two red cones, the sound of her heart beating in her ears. *Touchdown. Make the touchdown.*

Taylor hurdled over a defender who lunged for the flag flying from her waist and sailed past the cones.

"Touchdown!"

Her teammates raced to meet her, congratulating her with high fives.

Will busted through the group with a "Whoo hoo!" picked her up, and swung her around. "Taylor's *my* lady." He motioned to the rest of the guys. "My lady. Making touchdowns. Blowing past Jordan West."

Jordan protested with a deep huff, trying to catch his breath. "Taylor, next time, you play for me."

"Finders, keepers." Will wrapped his arm around her waist and pulled her to him.

Taylor stepped away from him. "Hello, I'm not a kept woman."

Jordan laughed and took the football from her. "Let's go, or we won't be able to finish before dark." He jogged over to his team.

Will caught Taylor's arm. "Sorry. I know that—"

"It's okay."

After the game, Will convinced Taylor to go for burgers and fries at Sam's. "Thanks for playing today. You made it fun. Bunch of smelly guys out on the field. . ." He winked at her. "Gets a little old."

"How often do you play?" she asked, taking a long sip from the straw in her water glass. She could see her red-faced reflection in Sam's shiny windows.

"Couple of times a month if the weather's good. Sometimes the guys have family stuff to do, or we're all at home taking naps."

She laughed then blurted, "Jordan asked me to dinner, Will."

He didn't flinch. "He's a nice guy."

"I have to be honest about something."

He picked up his soda glass. "There's more." His expression remained friendly, but his tone was defensive.

"I'm not staying in White Birch; you know that. I can't let our relationship go beyond casual friendship. I don't want to end up where we did ten years ago."

"A lot of things have changed since then."

"Of course," she said, her voice elevated. "But at the root of it all, we are in the exact same place now as then. You are married to Lambert's Furniture, and I'm married to. . .out there, getting my career back on track."

She stopped, not meaning to toss the marriage word into the conversation. She didn't mean to imply. . . "Not that we would, you know, want to get married, to each other, but I'm just saying. . ." She gazed up at Will. "Help?"

"What do you want me to say?"

She shrugged, frustrated. *He's been flirting with me for three weeks, and now he's acting like he's the one being cornered. So typical. Exactly what he did ten years ago.* "Forget it."

"Look, Taylor, you can have dinner with whoever you want."

"I'm aware of that. I just thought you should know."

"I appreciate it," he said, his smile forced.

They were silent for a long time. Taylor excused herself to go to the ladies' room where she splashed cold water on her face. Glancing in the mirror, she muttered, "Nice move, Hanson."

By the time she got back to the table, Will had evidently rebounded from her awkward attempt to expose any romantic undercurrents in their relationship.

"Taylor," he said, "I know we have a history. I know things didn't go the way either of us planned. But being with you the past few weeks has reminded me of how much I love being with you. How much I treasure your friendship."

"I'm sorry, Will. I didn't mean to be so rude." She stretched her hand out to his. "I love our friendship. You're one of the most amazing men I know."

"You are the most amazing woman I know."

She laughed. "I take it you don't know very many women."

He grew serious. "Let's just take it one day at a time."

"Perfect. Now can we order? I'm starved."

&

On Monday morning Will entered his brother's office. "I have an idea."

Bobby glanced up from his computer. "I'm shocked and amazed."

"Funny man." Will sat in the adjacent leather chair. "Let's hire Taylor."

"Hire Taylor?" Bobby shot Will a quizzical look. "For what?"

"The new business system. She's worked at two major New York CPA firms and one financial magazine. I'm sure she's been through this kind of conversion before." Will propped his forearms on his knees.

Bobby regarded him, tapping an unsharpened pencil on his desk. "It's really a brilliant idea. She's available, she's experienced, and she's extremely intelligent."

"We'd be crazy not to contract her. If she's willing."

"What does Ethan think?"

"Let's get him in here and find out."

Bobby picked up his phone and dialed Ethan.

"I was just on my way to see you two," Ethan said as he entered Bobby's office, taking the vacant seat next to Will. "One of the new CNC machines is giving us trouble. I called the vendor and they are coming out to replace it, but that means we're behind in production for a day or two. Which means our schedule will get backed up a week or more. We're already behind three weeks because of that lemon of a machine."

Will hung his head and pressed his palm against the back of his neck. "See if you can get some of the crew to work overtime until we're caught up. Let's pay double time."

Ethan whistled. "It's fair, but really going to hit our payroll budget hard."

Will laughed sardonically. "With that machine down, we're already off budget. Let's do what we can to make it up. Might as well throw in a comp day for every weekend day worked."

Ethan grinned. "They are going to love you, Boss."

"Speaking of love," Bobby said.

"Hey, no fair," Will said.

"Will wants to hire Taylor to consult on the HBS system. What do you think?"

Ethan looked at Will, then Bobby, grinning like he'd discovered a secret. "Fine by me."

"All right." Will stood. "I'll go see what the going rate is for consultants."

"Did you kiss her?" Ethan asked, still grinning.

Will stopped at Bobby's door. "If I did, I wouldn't tell you."

seven

Taylor ate breakfast with Dad and Mom in the warm, cozy kitchen, then spent the morning researching job opportunities.

By noon she was frustrated and anxious. She trotted down to the kitchen for a glass of water.

"How's it going?" Dad asked, tucking his newspaper away as she strolled into the family room.

She sat on the ottoman, in the rays of the sun streaming through the windows. "Terrible."

"Nothing turning up?"

She sipped her water and shook her head. "It's like I'm searching in the dark with absolutely no light. I'm so, so. . ." She stood. "Frustrated."

"I can see."

Taylor regarded him, thinking how well he looked after only a week. His cheeks had color, and his eyes sparkled.

"You can't let this get to you," Dad said. "Anxiety leads to depression, then you make bad decisions." He patted his stomach. "Look for the peace of Jesus right here. The peace that resonates from your spirit—not your head."

Taylor collapsed against the couch cushions and flopped her arm over her eyes. "Easy for you to say."

"No, I've had to work at walking in peace, too. Just like you and every other human on the planet."

"Except Will Adams."

"What do you mean?"

Taylor lifted her head to see her dad. "He exudes peace like he drinks a cup of it every morning for breakfast."

Dad laughed. "He does, but I know he's worked hard at walking in peace. He didn't get there overnight."

"Well, whatever he's got, I want it."

"You can have it."

"Yeah, I know. Be like Mary of Bethany, sitting at Jesus' feet."

"That's right. Settle your heart and mind on Jesus. Stay in prayer, meditating on God's Word. Marry Will."

Taylor jumped up. "Dad!"

"You won't find a better man, Taylor."

She drank from her water glass. "Maybe not, Dad, but he isn't asking." She hopped up and went to the kitchen.

The phone rang as she rounded the kitchen corner. She snatched up the receiver. "Hello?" She glanced at her dad, shaking her head. *Marry Will. Ha!*

"Taylor, Indiana Godwin."

She raised a brow. Indiana was the former head of human resources at Blankenship & Burns. "Indy, hello. How are you?"

"Doing well," he said. "Loving my life in Boston."

"Good for you. How did you know I was here?" Taylor asked.

"Reneé Ludwig sent me your résumé."

Taylor smiled, going to the refrigerator for more water. "She did?" She made a mental note to call Reneé and thank her.

"It's a stellar résumé."

Taylor leaned against the counter. "Thank you."

"I didn't know if you'd be interested in working for the Print First Newspaper Group."

Taylor raised a brow. Print First was one of the largest newspaper chains in the country. "I might be."

"It's a little different than what you're used to at a CPA firm, but you could handle a CFO or financial director position with no problem."

"Absolutely." Excitement bubbled in her middle.

"Unfortunately, we're going through a corporate restructure."

"I see." She filtered out a resonating disappointment. "You and every other company on the eastern seaboard."

"If you can hang on, I'm sure I can get you in for an interview by the New Year."

"Indy, that's three months away."

"I know, Taylor. Tell you what—let me talk to a few people and see what I can find. Maybe one of the smaller chains has a CFO position."

"Indiana, I appreciate it."

"You don't care where you live, do you?"

"No, but, Indy, the pay has to be right."

"I understand. Taylor, one more thing. This is kind of a delicate matter. . ."

She felt the blood drain from her face. "What? Tell me."

"Let me close my door."

Taylor heard the *kerplunk* of Indiana's office door. "I could get in big trouble for this, but as a friend, I need to tell you."

A prickly feeling ran over her scalp. Dread anchored her feet to the kitchen floor. "This doesn't sound good."

"We post all applications and résumés on the intranet. One of our VPs saw your résumé. Impressed, he decided to call Blankenship & Burns. He's one of those corporate big shots who thinks he can call up the White House and talk to the president if he wants."

Dread. Definitely dread. "Oh, no."

"He talked to your boss, Lisa Downey."

Taylor felt sick to her stomach. "Lisa and I clashed."

"No kidding. She told the VP all about it."

Taylor inhaled sharply. "Indy, she can't do that."

"I know that and you know that, but she did. I thought you should know. If any other companies call, she may vent to them, also."

Taylor sank to the floor, her head in her hands. "What am I going to do?"

"If I were you, I'd shoot her an e-mail or give her a call. Clear the air, if you know what I mean. But, Taylor, if you mention me, I'll deny it." He chuckled.

"I understand. Thank you."

"No problem. I talked to the vice president who called Lisa. I told him I knew you personally and surmised Lisa Downey was getting revenge."

Taylor laughed sardonically. "I can't believe this."

"What did happen up there, Taylor?"

Taylor sighed. "She is one of those women executives who don't like other women in management. She came down pretty hard on me, demanded a lot. In return, I subtly undermined her initiatives and authority."

"Welcome to corporate life."

"Yeah, but I don't want to play that way."

Taylor hung up. Angry and disappointed—more with herself than Lisa Downey—she went upstairs, put on her sneakers, and grabbed her sweatshirt. She needed to get out. Fresh air. Run. Think. Pray.

❧

Will slowed his truck, driving down Main Street after the town council meeting. In the bright afternoon light, farmers lined their produce carts along the south side of the city's center. Fresh apples, corn, squash, tomatoes, and crates of other fresh vegetables glistened in the sun.

Will glanced at his watch. Two o'clock and he was hungry for lunch. He spotted a fellow church deacon, Hank Burgraf, and waved. Next to him was a cousin on the Adams side, Lyle.

At the far end of the line, a vendor whipped cotton candy onto sticks for the moms out with their toddlers. Will shook his head, remembering the night with Mia. Verbal cotton candy.

He wanted to linger in town and grab a sandwich at Peri's, but he needed to get back to Lambert's Furniture. A pile of work waited on his desk.

Yet, when he cruised past Milo Park, Will parked. There wouldn't be many more days like today—sunny, blue skies with a gentle breeze—and he wanted to enjoy it while he could.

The walk to the park benches cleared his head, still stuffy from the council meeting. To build a skateboard park or not had been the big debate. Will saw the merits on both sides—for and against. However, when the discussion ran well past lunchtime, he motioned to table it until the next meeting.

Half the room shouted, "Second."

Now, taking long strides across the grounds, the mental cobwebs blew away, and Will caught sight of a familiar dark, burnished head. Taylor.

She sat with her face tipped to the sun, her sweatshirt balled between her hands in her lap. She'd been running.

"Beautiful day, isn't it?" Will said as he plopped down next to Taylor.

She screamed. He laughed. She popped him lightly on the arm.

"Ouch." He rubbed the spot.

"You scared the wits out of me."

He laughed. "I doubt that."

"What are you doing in the park in the middle of the afternoon?"

Will stretched out and crossed his legs at the ankles. He locked his hands behind his head and closed his eyes. "Town council meeting every Monday."

"Ah."

"What are you doing?"

"Praying. Well, trying to pray, but I'm sulking more than anything else."

He tipped his face upward. "What's going on?"

"Stuff."

He opened one eye. "Like what?"

Starting with a sigh, Taylor told him about the call from Indiana Godwin, the wonderful job possibility, and how her track record with Lisa Downey followed her.

Will thought for a moment. "I've learned there are always two sides to every story. This Lisa person must feel justified in some way."

"Whose side are you on?" Taylor jumped to her feet and walked back and forth in front of the bench.

"Yours, of course. But you're not going to get Lisa Dowling—"

"Downey."

"Downey—to admit any wrongs."

"So I'm helpless? At the mercy of her opinion?"

Will squinted up at her, catching the ire in her eyes. "No. But sulking over her isn't going to change anything. You've got to take the higher road. Don't let some woman hundreds of miles away in New York control your emotions."

She lifted her arms in surrender. "You're right; you're right."

Will patted the park bench. "Sit."

"No, I'm too antsy."

"Sit!"

Taylor sat. "I feel like your dog, Harry."

"No," Will said with a shake of his head, "he sits the first time I tell him."

"Ha, ha."

Will grabbed her hand. "Can I pray with you?"

Taylor bowed her head, her lips moving in silent prayer. Will noticed her grip grew tighter and tighter.

"Father, Taylor wants Your best. Give her wisdom and peace. Let her know the plans You have for her. I know You delight in her."

A drop of moisture hit his hand. Taylor sniffled then covered her face with her free hand. Will wrapped her in his arms. When her tears subsided, he gave her his handkerchief.

"Better?"

She laughed and blew her nose. "Much. Thanks." She faced him, her eyes and nose red. "I've been mad at Lisa for being an ogre when all along I should have been asking for forgiveness for my own selfish actions."

"Now it's forgotten. Over."

"Well, I probably need to e-mail or call Lisa, but yes, the Lord's forgiven me." Taylor carefully folded the handkerchief and tucked it in her pocket. "I'll wash it for you."

Will grinned and smoothed his hand over her hair. "It's going to be all right, Taylor Jo."

She leaned against him, and his hand cradled her shoulder. "Sure, but my career is still stopped at the red light of life. I need a green go."

"In that case, I have a proposal for you."

eight

To her surprise, the word *proposal* made her skin tingle. In an instant, time rolled back and she stood with Will on the White Birch covered bridge, serenaded by the water and surrendering her heart to love.

". . .installing a new business system. We can't go forward with our e-business until we can handle the revenue and reporting."

Taylor tuned in to Will. "Um, what? Business system?"

He grinned, making her feel like they were the only two people in existence. He had a way about him that made her feel special. "Right. We're looking at HBS—"

She perked up at the familiar initials. "Hayes Business Systems?"

"Yes."

"Very classy. Kind of high-end for Lambert's Furniture, don't you think?"

"For now, but we've developed a line of furniture to sell online. HBS has a great solution for e-businesses including a module to work with online and distributor inventories."

"They do. But, Will, a lot of their standard modules are very expensive and over the top for the streamlined business you run. Even with adding the e-business, you'll—"

He held up his hand. "Taylor, this is exactly why I—we—want to hire you. Work for us as a consultant. Help us pick the right solution and installation process."

"Work for Lambert's Furniture?"

"Yes." He stood, arms out to the side, his expression like he'd discovered genius.

"I don't know, Will." She regarded him, wondering how it would feel to work every day with him. Her goal was to fix her career debacle, not lose herself in White Birch and fall in love, again, with Will Adams. "My career is important to me."

Will tipped his head to one side. "Consulting for a multimillion-dollar furniture company would look nice on a résumé."

She glanced up at him, squinting in the sunlight. "Can I pray about it?"

He knelt in front of her, forearms propped on his knees. "Absolutely."

❧

Taylor wandered upstairs to her room, her thoughts a million miles away.

"Taylor, is that you?" Mom knocked lightly on the bedroom door and peeked inside.

"It's me." Taylor kissed her on the cheek. "You look happy."

"Your dad just beat me at Scrabble." Her delicate smile fanned the tiny lines of her cheeks and around her eyes. "Dinner will be ready in an hour."

"Need help?" Taylor grabbed clothes to wear after her shower.

Mom waved both hands. "No. Go visit with your dad. He's in the library." She started down the stairs. "Tim, Dana, and the kids are coming tonight."

"That'll liven things up."

After her shower, Taylor knocked on the library door, her hair still wet.

"Come in," Dad called. "Did you have a nice run?" He closed his Bible.

"I did." Taylor sat on the window seat. She loved the library. It was bright from the southern exposure and cozy with its overstuffed Lambert's Furniture chair, ottoman, and a rocker. This was Tim's old room, but after he married Dana, Dad knocked out a wall to make a library.

"Will offered me a job," she said.

Dad stood and stretched. "Really?"

Taylor stared out the window. "He wants me to consult on the purchase of a new business system."

Dad joined her on the window seat. "They've been wanting to upgrade for a long time."

Taylor looked at him. His cheeks were pink again, his eyes bright. "Should I do it?"

"If you want," Dad said, his words even, not hinting of a yes or a no.

"What about my career?"

"What about it?"

Taylor stood, feet apart, arms folded. "If I work for Lambert's, I'll get caught up in the job, give a hundred and ten percent, and forget to keep looking *out there.*" She motioned toward the window. She felt like a stuck record, repeating the same mantra, but she felt driven to land a CPA position with a lucrative firm.

"It's a consulting job, Taylor. A good line for your résumé. Unaccounted-for time is a negative, you know." Dad regarded her for a moment. "Still hurts, does it?"

"What still hurts?" She walked over to the desk where faded black and white photographs lined the edges.

"Losing Will."

Remembering pressed her emotions to the surface. "Yes," she said quietly. "Which is crazy after ten years."

She picked up a gold-framed picture of her parents on their wedding day in 1960. They smiled in black and white, walking up the church aisle, holding hands. That's what she had wanted with Will. But he wasn't ready.

Dad stood behind her now. "I almost lost your mom." He chuckled as he remembered. "She was a feisty one."

Taylor whirled round, the picture still in her hands. "Who, pixie Trixie?"

Dad gave her a deep nod. "Your grandpa insisted she marry into money and culture. Bringing home a common laborer from the furniture mill didn't fit Raymond's idea of a suitable husband for his little girl."

Taylor sat against the desk. "I never heard this. What'd you do?"

"Never gave up. Prayed a lot, as I recall. Did what I had to do to convince her father she'd have a wonderful life with me. For a while she dated Lem Maher down in Boston. I almost lost her then."

"Lem Maher of Maher Stationary and Business Supplies?"

"That'd be the one."

"Wow, Dad. Pretty *rico* competition." She rolled the *r* in *rico*.

He winked. "Love conquers all. Even money."

She put the picture back and crossed her arms. "And the moral to this story is?" She furrowed her brow.

Dad returned to his chair. "Not sure. Maybe there's a reason you and Will aren't married—to each other or anyone else. Maybe there's a reason you quit your job and moved home. Maybe there's a reason you showed up just when Will needed help with a new business system. Maybe there's a reason he asked you to help him. Maybe there's a reason you should say yes."

Taylor looked at him, a wry twist on her lips. "Aren't you full of reason tonight?"

Mom called up the stairs. "Grant, the kids are here. Taylor. . ."

Dad walked toward the door. "I can see lots of reasons why you should work for Lambert's Furniture. Least of all, finding out if you still love Will."

Taylor stopped him before he walked out. "I don't want to fall in love with him, Dad. It's over, too late."

He kissed her cheek. "Then don't. But do the job. Don't cut off your nose to spite your face."

❧

For Will, matters of the heart confounded him. They were confusing and complicated. He liked specific processes and procedures, clear-cut goals with achievable results. Why couldn't falling in love be like earning his MBA, running a business, or making furniture?

Instead, he had to navigate the minefield of Taylor's emotions. He had no map of her heart or his, no blueprint, no how-to manual. No way to know if he trod on dangerous ground.

Loving Taylor fell into a completely different category than loving his family and friends—the category of *difficult and hard.* Because if she didn't love him back, he didn't know what he would do.

Will pondered his relationship with Taylor as he parked his truck at Lambert's Furniture and trekked to the office door.

Did he love Taylor? After ten years? It didn't make sense, but then matters of the heart never did.

Will checked Bobby's office as he walked by. "I saw Taylor. Made my proposal."

Bobby reclined in his chair. "And?"

"She's praying about it."

"Does she know you proposed a job, not marriage?" Bobby asked.

"Funny."

Bobby walked around his desk and shut his office door. "Got a minute?"

Will took a chair. "I know what you're going to say, Bob."

"Then why don't you do something about it?"

Will gazed at the ceiling for a second, thinking. Slowly he shook his head. "I'm not sure."

"Do you know how unlikely it is for a beautiful, intelligent woman like Taylor to be available and in town just when you're finally ready to settle down?"

"She wants a career, Bob. She always has."

"She wants you. She always has."

Will regarded him. "Not anymore. She told me."

"Told you what?" Bobby asked.

"That I'm married to Lambert's Furniture and she's married to *out there*." He pointed at nothing. "Besides, she's going on a date with Jordan West." Will shook his head. How could he even consider the notion that he might be in love with her?

Bobby nudged him. "Since when did *no* ever stop you?"

Will rubbed his forehead. "You sound like Grandpa."

Bobby grinned. "Thanks."

Will thought for a moment, rubbing his chin, then said, "I guess I could tell you now. After all, it's been ten years."

"Tell me what?" Bobby waited.

"What happened after your wedding reception."

A light rap on the door interrupted the story before it began. Ethan stuck his head inside. "Will, Martin Leslie's on the phone again. He really wants to talk to you about his last shipment."

Will slapped his hands against his knees and stood. "I'm on my way."

Bobby patted his shoulder as he passed. "We can talk later. See you at the grandparents' tonight?"

Will paused in the doorway. "I'll be there."

❧

Taylor read her e-mail to Lisa Downey one last time. Short and to the point, she simply apologized for her attitude during her final days at Blankenship & Burns.

> *It was never my intent to hurt you or your department. My actions and attitude were unprofessional. Please forgive me.*
>
> *Sincerely,*
> *Taylor Hanson*

She moved the cursor to the SEND button. Praying, she hesitated a second.

She didn't expect Lisa Downey to change her mind—or respond with her own apology. Taylor merely wanted to close a door she'd left ajar.

"Lord, here goes." She clicked SEND.

Downstairs, laughter reverberated from the family room where her parents played a board game with Tim, Dana, and the boys, Quentin and Jarred.

As Taylor came down, feeling like a weight had been lifted, she winked at Claire who was ending a conversation on her cell phone.

"What's up, Aunt Taylor?" she asked, clicking her phone shut.

Taylor smiled. "Not much." She sat on the edge of the ottoman.

"Can I ask you a question?" Claire flopped against the couch cushions.

"Sure."

"If you cared about someone but they didn't care for you, what would you do?"

Taylor squared her shoulders, thoughtful. "Boy or girl?"

Claire hesitated. "Boy."

"How long have you, or *someone*, cared about the guy?"

Claire pinched her lips together then muttered, "Awhile."

"Well, the new wisdom of today is if a guy is into you, he'll let you know."

Claire nodded. "That's true."

"Otherwise, move on. Don't waste your time on a guy who's not treating you like you're queen of the universe. Move to New York, get a job, work yourself to death."

Claire laughed. "Like you?"

Taylor winced. "Yes, like me."

"Dad said Will Adams broke your heart."

The words punched up old feelings. "Yeah, well, your dad says a lot of things."

Claire moved to the ottoman. "What should I do?"

"Who is he?"

She shrugged. "Some guy from White Birch Community College."

"Claire, if I were you, here's what I'd do. Go home and write down all the ways you think you should be treated. Be real and honest. Write down how the Lord would want you to be treated. Your parents. Your friends. And if the guy doesn't measure up, he's not for you."

"His loss?" Claire asked, her voice weak and unsure.

"Yes, his loss," Taylor repeated, strong and sure, then kissed Claire's forehead. "You're too beautiful and precious to me, your parents, Grandma, Grandpa, and especially the Lord. Don't let any guy treat you like you're not."

From the family room, Tim called for Claire to join the game.

"In a minute, Dad," she answered.

"Sounds like he's getting clobbered," Taylor said, smiling.

"Probably. Can I ask you something else, Aunt Taylor?"

"Shoot."

"Why'd you quit your job? Dad said you loved it and loved life in New York."

Taylor laughed. "See, I told you your dad says a lot of things."

Claire giggled. "He does."

"Claire, sometimes you have to let go of one dream to realize another."

"Claire, help," Tim called again.

"You'd better go." Taylor nudged her niece.

"What is your other dream?" Claire asked, standing.

Taylor regarded her. "I'll let you know when I wake up."

Claire smiled and hurried to partner with her father, and Taylor went to the kitchen for the cordless phone. Breathing deeply, she dialed.

On the other end, the answering machine picked up.

"Will, hi, it's Taylor. I guess you're not home 'cause I'm talking to your machine. Thank you for your job offer. I'd be honored to help Lambert's Furniture. I can start Wednesday."

nine

"Come on, help me." Grandpa tapped Will on the shoulder. "Need more wood for the fire."

Will pushed away from the dinner table. "Thanks for dinner, Grandma. It was delicious as usual."

"Pineapple upside-down cake coming up next."

Outside in the cold, Will helped Grandpa gather logs.

"I like the direction you're taking the business, Will." Grandpa huffed and puffed a little as he hoisted a large log.

"Glad you approve."

"Hiring Taylor was smart."

"It's only an offer right now. It would be a huge blessing to have her experience and expertise on this project."

"For more reasons than one," Grandpa said, grinning as he dusted off his hands. "We've got enough wood. Let's go in."

"Grandpa, that's the only reason."

Grandpa opened the kitchen door. "If you say so." He shook his head.

"It's not that simple." Will dropped the wood by the fireplace, thinking how everyone oversimplified his relationship with Taylor. He tossed another large log onto the fire.

As he dusted bits of dirt and wood from his hands, Will's cousin Elizabeth approached. "Here, your arms look empty. I'm going to help Grandma." She handed him her one-year-old son, Matthew.

Will held the squirming child in the crook of his arm. When Matthew's father, Kavan, came around the corner, he laughed.

"Whoa, Will, he's not a football." Kavan set the boy upright.

Will grinned and glanced self-consciously around the room. "It's been a long time since I held a baby."

Ethan and Julie flopped onto the couch with plates of cake. "Looking good, Will. Thinking about getting one of those?" Ethan asked.

"He needs a wife first," Will's dad, Buddy, said.

Will held up his free hand. "Stop." He tried to jiggle little Matt to prove how good he was with children, but the little boy simply cried.

Julie stood, reaching her arms out. "Hand him over."

As more of the family gathered around the fire and talk of marriage and babies increased, Will stepped out. He needed to think.

The night was dark, but he knew his way down to the covered bridge without a light. The wind blew against his face, sharp and cold, until he reached the cover of the old bridge.

"Lord, all this pressure about Taylor. . ." He leaned against the weatherworn walls, hands in his pockets.

Suddenly, a small circle of light flashed across the bridge. "Grandma sent me down with this." Bobby held up a steaming mug of coffee.

Will grinned, reaching for the large cup. "It was getting crowded in there."

Bobby propped himself next to Will. "They just want you to be happy."

"Who says I'm not?"

"Well, they mean married happy."

"Naturally."

Bobby ran the flashlight's beam along the bridge's rafters. "I carved mine and Elle's initials right over there, I think, the night we got engaged."

Will's gaze followed the beam. "I don't think there's any room up there for more initials."

Bobby laughed. "You get engaged, I'll find room."

"Two miracles in one night. Don't know if the world could take it."

"What happened the night of my wedding?" Bobby asked.

Will sipped his coffee. He'd been expecting the question.

How strange to share it now after so many years.

"Taylor and I came up here to the bridge. Maybe it was the romance of the moon, maybe it was your wedding, but love was in the air. Definitely in the air."

"I remember it was really warm that night. We had an outdoor reception and all I wanted was to leave with Elle and get into air-conditioning." Bobby laughed. "Seems so stupid now."

Will continued, the memory awakened. "Taylor wanted to go wading. We didn't have a flashlight. I had on my tux. She had on her bridesmaid's dress."

"Sounds like fun."

"We laughed so hard, I fell in. She tore the hem of her dress and stubbed her toe on a rock. When I tried to drive her home, my old orange Camaro wouldn't start, so we walked to Mom and Dad's."

"That's five miles, Will."

"I know. I carried her piggyback for half of it. She had on these funky shoes that were impossible to walk in." Recalling the picture made him laugh out loud.

"So, what went wrong?"

Will picked up the story. "I knew I was in love with her. But I started grad school in the fall, and I wanted to be focused. Besides, all she ever talked about was living in Manhattan. I didn't think we were ready for the kind of love I was feeling."

"And you told her?"

Will looked out into the darkness, the coffee mug warm in his hand. "Are you kidding? I had the safe plan: Say nothing. Of course, I kissed her, which didn't help."

"What happened next?" Bob prodded.

"I got the keys to Dad's car and took her home. By then our feelings were so raw and out there, we didn't say anything. I've never, ever felt like that before or since. I knew I couldn't even kiss her again, 'cause if I did. . ." He stopped and drew a deep breath. "When I pulled into the Hansons' drive, she leaned over, told me she loved me, and. . ."

Will stopped. How could such an old memory provoke such a new love?

"Hey, don't leave me hanging."

"She asked me to marry her."

Bobby choked. "What?"

Will tossed out the last of his coffee and strolled down the length of the bridge. "She wanted to elope to New York—get married."

"Wow, I can't imagine Taylor laying her heart on the line like that."

Will shook his head. "I told you love was in the air."

"I take it your response wasn't 'Yeah, let's go!'"

Will laughed. "No. I didn't say anything for a long time. Too long. Finally, I babbled something about going to grad school. Never told her I loved her. Or that I would like to marry her someday. She jumped out of the car, ran inside, and the next day she was gone."

Bobby stood next to him on the edge of the bridge, shining the flashlight across the barren treetops. "And you didn't go after her?"

Will mumbled, "No," then added, "I thought I would, eventually. Eventually never came."

"You are one lucky man." Bobby shone the flashlight on Will's face. "Somehow, ten years later, *eventually* came to you."

❧

Taylor knocked on Will's office door. "Taylor Hanson reporting for work."

Will hopped up, sloshing coffee over the rim of his cup. "Good morning. Come in."

The heels of her designer pumps thudded against the hardwood floor.

Will regarded her for a moment. "You look nice," he said with a low whistle. "A little overkill, but very nice."

Taylor ran her hand down the front of her five-hundred-dollar suit. "This is a professional arrangement, is it not?"

Their eyes met, and she wondered if he could see right through her to her rapidly beating heart.

Will stuttered. "Of course, but you don't need an expensive suit to impress the bosses around here."

She cleared her throat and glanced at the floor. "I'll keep that in mind." Why did it seem as if they were talking about more than her job at Lambert's Furniture?

"Let me show you to your office."

Taylor followed Will. He introduced her to some of the administrative and financial staff, though she already knew most of them.

"Markie, good to see you." Taylor shook the hand of her old friend.

"Taylor, welcome home."

"Well, home for now." She felt shy about admitting her career failure. No matter how wonderful home might feel, it was a temporary stop.

"Here you go." Will opened the door, and Taylor stepped into a large, windowed office with a long, polished mahogany desk surrounded by old leather chairs. And in the corner, a stone fireplace beckoned.

"Will, it's beautiful."

"It's the old conference room. When we added the south wing we built a new one."

Taylor set her shoulder bag on the desk. "Are you sure you want me in here? This looks like a CEO's office."

Will perched on the desk's edge. "It's your office now. By the way, I didn't have time to get you any equipment." He motioned around the room. "No computer."

"I'm going to need one of those." Taylor winked at him, her hands on her hips. She liked being here, though the idea of being near Will both thrilled and terrified her. How he'd captivated her heart after all these years mystified her.

"We have about five thousand in the capital budget for a computer and software purchases, so—"

"That's a good start. But save that extra money for training. All I need is a fast computer and a connection to the Internet."

"We can handle that." Will pulled out a chair and sat, then

brought Taylor up to speed on their business plan and how a new system fit into their strategy.

"I think HBS is a good choice, Will. I just want to make sure you don't get stuck with a bunch of modules you don't need," Taylor said when he finished.

She pulled her data assistant out of her case and made a note. "I know a few businesses who use HBS. I can give them a call."

Will nodded. "Bobby's been talking to an HBS sales rep, so you should get with him."

Taylor agreed, making more notes. "We should get them in here for a demo again and talk about your needs."

"Taylor, take the lead on this. Just tell us when and where."

Taylor tipped her head to one side. "I will. I'll get with Markie to see how things flow in the office and design a workflow and project plan. I can do that while I'm waiting for my computer to arrive."

Will was grinning at her.

"What?" she said.

"I like this side of you. Very in command."

She stared at him. If only he knew her insides were quivering like cold gelatin and if she weren't sitting in his place of business she'd want to kiss him. She cleared her throat and shook the image from her mind. "I'll need a computer to order my computer."

Will laughed. "My office."

Taylor scratched Harry's ears as she took Will's desk chair. He sniffed her shoes and wagged his tail.

Will gathered a stack of papers. "I'll be in the conference room."

She swallowed and smiled. "And I'll be here."

He paused at the door. "Markie is drawing up your contract. I researched the going consultant rates, but if it's too low, let me know."

Taylor waved off his remark. "I'm sure it's a fair wage." Besides, she wasn't really doing this for the money.

He nodded, grinned, and left. She slumped down in his chair, the aroma of clean soap floating around her. *I can't do this, Lord. I can't. I'm falling in love with him.*

Harry nudged her leg as if he understood her thoughts. Taylor stroked his head and sighed.

❦

For the tenth time in ten minutes, Will read the last line of their contract with Martin Leslie & Company. Thoughts of Taylor seemed way more intriguing than a distributor's contract.

He glanced at his watch. Ten o'clock. The coffeepot in the corner sat empty. Will shoved away from the conference table and dug in his pocket for change to get coffee from the production floor vending machine. No, no, what he needed was a cup of Peri's rich, special blend.

He headed to his office for his keys, suspecting he wanted an excuse to see Taylor more than he wanted a cup of Peri's best. But his chair was empty and disappointment twanged in his chest. He reached for his jacket and called to Harry. "Let's go for a ride."

Outside, early November snowflakes surprised him. It was too early for snow. But soft white flakes floated down over him. Then he heard screaming and. . .giggling?

He stepped to the side of the building, and there was Taylor, in her fancy periwinkle blue suit, catching snowflakes on her tongue with Markie.

Will guffawed. Harry barked.

"Laugh at us, will you?" Markie lobbed a tiny, powdery snowball at Will. It fell apart in midair.

Will laughed harder while Harry ran in circles, barking.

Out of nowhere, Taylor shouted, "Charge!" and ran for Will.

He tried to run, but his loafers provided no traction. Before he knew it, Taylor grabbed his collar and slipped an icy concoction down his back.

"Ahh! Cold. Cold." He whipped around, grasping at her.

She tried to escape, but running in heels proved impossible. She slipped, arms flailing. Will scooped her up in his arms just as his feet slipped out from under him. They went sprawling to the ground.

Unable to stop laughing, Markie stood over them, shivering, her hands grasping her waist. "I haven't done this since I was about ten, Taylor. Thanks, but I'm wet, freezing, and going inside."

Will helped Taylor to her feet.

"Ouch. I hurt," he said.

She laughed, adding, "I think I twisted my ankle."

He looked into her green eyes. "Are you okay?"

She nodded, dusting white powder from her suit. Her feet slipped again, and she fell against him. With her face inches from his, their eyes met.

He cleared his throat and stepped away, holding her steady with one hand on her elbow. "Can you stand?"

She jerked her suit jacket into place and smoothed her wet hair. "I think so." She hiccupped a giggle.

Will felt lost in time and space. He couldn't breathe. "You need help to the door?" he croaked. The moment was charged with emotion.

"I should change my clothes." She inched forward slowly. "So much for impressing the bosses."

"I can drive you home." He pulled his keys from his pocket and pushed the remote access button. The alarm chirped and the lights flashed.

"No, thanks. I'll take my car."

He started to protest, but one look told him her guard was up. "Would you like me to bring back coffee from Peri's?"

She paused at the door. "Yes, thank you. A large fat-free latte?"

He nodded, striking the air with keys in hand. "One fat-free latte."

ten

As the gray day faded to black, a fresh snow fell. Taylor glanced at her watch then massaged the back of her neck.

"Calling it a night?" Will stood in her doorway.

"I guess so. It's six thirty. I'm getting a little hungry."

"Can I buy you dinner?"

Taylor shook her head. It took her most of the afternoon to get rid of the image of him holding her, a dusting of snow on his head and shoulders. "Mom has lasagna waiting."

Will's eyes widened with a twinkle. "Trixie makes a mean lasagna."

Taylor shut down her laptop, which she'd brought from home to use for the afternoon. Her parents would love to see him. But she'd made it clear they were just friends. If they kept hanging around together, everything would get confused.

But when she looked up at him, she said, "I'm sure Mom wouldn't mind setting another plate."

Clicking off the office light, Taylor walked with Will to her car. She dropped her laptop into the passenger seat, then regarded him for a moment. "Thank you. For the job."

"You're welcome." He slipped his arm around her waist.

Her back stiffened, and she pressed her hands against his chest. Though, inside, she felt like a toasted marshmallow. "I guess we'd better get going."

"Taylor, I. . ." He looked into her eyes, tipped his head, then slowly touched his lips to hers, tenderly but with passion.

The kiss ended too soon. Caught up in the moment, Taylor couldn't speak. She cleared her throat and muttered, "Wow."

He laughed and kissed her forehead. "Is that a good wow?"

She stepped around him and slipped into her car. "See you at the house."

"Yeah, see you there," Will said, shutting her door shut and walked to his truck. In the side mirror, she watched him, tears stinging in her eyes. She couldn't love him again. She wouldn't.

She cried for several minutes; then she pulled herself together and drove home. But by the time she parked in the driveway, her tears had given way to ire.

Will parked his truck behind her. She jerked open the car door and stepped out.

"Don't you ever kiss me like that again," she said, pointing at Will as he walked toward her.

He didn't flinch. "I meant that kiss."

In the porch light, she could see the solid lines of his face. His warm breath smelled like mints. "I don't care what you meant, Will. Don't ever, ever kiss me like that again."

"I'm in love with you." He settled against her car.

In the cold, her voice rang out like bells. "Ha! In love with me? You're not in love with me; you're in love with a memory."

"No, I'm in love with you. Always have been."

She laughed, slapping her hand on her forehead. "Oh, right, I forgot. You wanted to marry me, but I said no. Then you chased me all over New York begging me to reconsider. But finally, you gave up and came home to run Lambert's Furniture."

He straightened away from the car. "Good night." He pulled his keys out of his pocket.

"Where are you going?"

"Home."

Taylor trembled, but not from the cold or the snow gathering on her hair and shoulders. His control irritated her. Deep down, she wanted him to fight this out—to fight for her.

"I loved you." She gestured at him with her arm.

He walked back toward her. "I was—am—in love with you, but I wasn't ready for marriage ten years ago. Neither were you."

"Then why didn't you say something?"

His jaw muscle tightened. "I thought it would be better left unsaid."

She growled and turned away, her hands balled into fists.

"It took me three years to stop thinking of you night and day. Every man I dated I compared to you."

"I never stopped thinking about you."

She whirled around. "Then why are we here on the other side of a decade? Why didn't you call or write or stop by when I came home for a visit? It's not like I lived on the other side of the country or the other side of the world."

He reached for her. "I don't know. But, Taylor, you're here now, and I know what I want. Let's get it right in this decade."

"It's too late," she whispered.

The front door opened, and Mom stepped into a sliver of yellow light. "Will, Taylor, come in, dinner's waiting."

Will touched her cheek lightly with the back of his hand. "I'll go on home."

Taylor touched his hand. "Don't go." She rubbed her forehead with her cold fingers. "If you leave, Mom will ask a million questions."

Will chuckled wryly. "I suppose the tension between us won't make her suspicious at all."

"Trixie Hanson will be so glad to have you at her table she won't notice." Taylor reached into the BMW's backseat for her laptop case and handbag.

Will followed her up the walkway. "This conversation isn't over."

Taylor murmured, "No, I guess it isn't."

When the hallway clock cuckooed at nine, Will stood, declared Grant the king of chess, and said, "I need to go home while I still have some dignity."

Grant slapped his knee. "I was about to checkmate."

Will grinned. "I know."

Taylor watched from the chaise chair where she sat curled up with the *New York Times* and the *Boston Globe*.

"Anything interesting?" Will asked, stopping by her chair.

Grant walked past, calling to his wife, "Trixie, Will's leaving."

Taylor answered without looking up. "Lots of things. Mostly

keeping up on the stock market."

Will moved the folded front page of the *Times* so he could sit on the arm of the chair. "I'm sorry—"

"It was lovely to have you tonight, Will." Trixie held out his coat, her perfect smile lighting her petite face.

"Thank you, Trixie. Dinner was delicious."

"Oh, let me wrap up some for you to take home." She handed Will's coat to her husband and bustled out of the family room toward the kitchen.

Grant gave Will his coat. "I think I'll get some ice cream," he said and left the room.

Will considered his next words to Taylor since he was sure he only had a few seconds before Grant and Trixie returned. "I didn't mean to upset you."

"I know you didn't."

He looked across the room. "So, where does this leave us?"

"I don't know."

"Here you go, Will." Trixie handed him a square plastic container.

"You spoil me," he said, taking the lasagna and giving her a light hug. "Thank you."

"You've been so good to Grant." She stood perfectly straight, her hands clasped together.

"We like to take care of our *family*."

Grant hollered from the kitchen, "I can't find the ice cream scoop."

Trixie excused herself.

Taylor stared in the direction of the kitchen. "Dad's addicted to ice cream. It's his kryptonite."

Will pulled on his coat. "I probably fell in love with you over a scoop of chocolate in a sugar cone."

"I suppose so," she said.

He wondered when she fell in love with him but didn't ask. "Would you like to get some ice cream?"

She looked up. "Now?"

He shrugged. "Sure."

She shook her head. "It's late—and snowing. I'll pass."

He nodded. "See you tomorrow then?"

"Yes." Taylor flipped the edges of the newspaper.

"When are you. . ." He stopped.

"Going to dinner with Jordan?"

He nodded.

"Friday."

"Good night, Taylor," he said, turning to leave then paused. "See you tomorrow."

She looked at him. "Yes, see you tomorrow."

Driving home, Will prayed, sorry his kiss caused such a quarrel. But he loved her. He knew that now, and he wouldn't give up until she loved him, too.

❧

Jordan tried too hard, in Taylor's opinion. He reeked of cologne, his hair glistened with too much gel, and his normally graceful gait looked stiff and robotic.

He stared straight ahead the entire movie, and when they left the theater with hordes of other White Birch citizens, they walked to his car in silence.

Where was the fun, relaxed Jordan from the football game?

"Sorry about the mess," he said, moving more of his football gear to the backseat. A teacher, Jordan used his car as an office, or so it seemed to Taylor.

"What subjects do you teach?"

"I teach Phys Ed, of course, and I coach. I also teach a couple of history classes. I'm a little bit of a buff, as they say."

"What's your favorite historical time?" Taylor asked, settling in the passenger seat. The hinge moaned and squeaked as Jordan shoved the passenger door closed.

"World War One. It's an interesting time in world history," Jordan said when he got in his side of the car. "I've always loved the mystique behind Teddy Roosevelt."

"Yes, he's a fascinating man."

He placed his arm between the bucket seats, his right hand on the headrest behind her, and stared at her for a second. Taylor fidgeted with her hands and wished he'd start the engine.

She thought he might kiss her, so she moved back an inch.

He touched her shoulder and asked, "Where to now?"

She shrugged and quickly glanced at the dash clock. Nine thirty. "Where would you like to go?" She hated to suggest home already.

"Peri's Perk is a fun place on Friday nights. Lots of the town folks out, and there's usually a guitar player."

She smiled. "Sounds good."

It was late when Will left Lambert's Furniture. He didn't bother checking on Taylor. She'd worked late most nights this week, but he knew she had a date tonight.

He tried not to picture Jordan laughing and talking with her, looking into her green eyes. His cell phone chirped. "Hello."

"Hello, son, it's Grandpa."

Will unlocked his truck, hunching against the icy night wind. "What's up?"

"Grandma thought you might want some dinner."

Will laughed. "As a matter of fact, I do." He'd been planning to stop by anyway. He needed advice.

When Will entered the Lamberts' home on the hill, he hung his coat by the kitchen door. Next to the oven, Grandma stirred batter in a large bowl.

She smiled at him. "Let me get you a bowl of chili and a couple slices of warm bread."

Will kissed her on the cheek. "They don't make them like you anymore."

Her blue eyes sparkled. "I hear they're making them prettier and taller these days. Skinnier, too."

Will shook his head. "Just cheap imitations."

She laughed. "Scoot. Go see your grandpa."

In the living room, Grandpa swayed back and forth in his rocker. "How are things with your new consultant?"

"Worth every penny we've been paying her," Will said. "She's already saved us ten thousand dollars on the HBS deal."

Grandpa chuckled. "Not surprised to hear that."

"Here you go, Will." Grandma set a tray with steaming chili and hot, buttered bread on the coffee table. "What do you want to drink?"

Will shrugged. "Whatever you got. Water's fine."

"How about tea? Hot or iced?"

Will looked up at her. "Iced tea is good, but you don't have to wait on me, Grandma."

She fluttered out of the room. "Of course I do."

Grandpa regarded him. "What's on your mind?"

Will scooted to the edge of the couch, stirring the chili, letting it cool. "How did you win the heart of the prettiest lady in White Birch?"

Grandpa belly-laughed. "You're asking me?"

"Yes." Will slurped a spoonful of chili. Still too hot.

Leaning forward, Grandpa said, "I had the sympathy, man-in-uniform angle going for me."

Will laughed. "Are you telling me if it weren't for World War II, I might not be here?"

"There's a real possibility." Grandpa's smile seemed to make his dark eyes twinkle. "You'd better talk to your grandma about winning over a woman's heart."

"What's this?" Grandma came in with a tall glass of tea.

"Will needs our help, Betty."

She sat down and placed her hands in her lap. "You got ten minutes. Cookies are in the oven."

Will laughed. "Tell me how to win Taylor. She thinks our time has passed. Too late. Lost what we once had."

Grandma waved her hand. "Taylor's easy, Will. She already loves you. I can see it in her eyes. You just need to let her know that no matter what, you're going to be there for her. Never let her go. Prove whatever happened between you ten years ago won't happen again."

Will grinned. Simple. Wise. Brilliant. Hopefully, not impossible.

eleven

"Well, well. Will Adams, we meet again." Mia Wilmington sashayed down the aisle toward him just as he tossed a forty-pound bag of dog food to his shoulder.

"Mia. Hello." He smiled but felt awkward seeing her again.

"What are you doing at Sinclair's alone on a Friday night? A man like you ought to have a pretty woman on his arm."

He agreed. But at the moment she was out with Jordan West. Pointing to the bag on his shoulder, he answered her question. "Dog needs food."

"How sweet. Is there anything more romantic than a man who loves animals?" Mia tapped his arm with her well-manicured hand and batted her thick eyelashes.

He took a step back. "I suppose there are lots of things."

She chortled. "Oh, you. Listen, let's go for a coffee or something."

"No, I'd better get home."

"Oh, come on now. Don't leave me hanging. You never did call after our date."

Will winced. He didn't mean to be rude to Mia, but he knew his affections belonged to Taylor.

"Well. . ."

"Come on, be a sport."

"I guess one cup of coffee with a friend would be all right." While he enjoyed Grandma's chili, a cup of Peri's coffee would top off his night.

"Sure, friend," she said coyly.

❧

Jordan held open the door to Peri's. "Can you believe this weather?" Jordan asked, picking the first available table.

"Cold for November, isn't it?" Taylor shivered and tucked her hands under her arms, breathing in the heady scent of blended coffees and teas and something that smelled like grilled bread.

Jordan offered to take her coat, but she declined. "Need to warm up for a second."

"Sorry that old beater of mine doesn't have better heat. I'd buy a new car, but I'm building a house, so all my money is tied up."

Taylor nodded and smiled. "How nice. A new house."

"Yeah, it's been a dream for a long time. Shall we order?" Jordan jumped to his feet. "What'll it be? Coffee, latte, tea?"

"Hot chocolate. Large. Extra hot," Taylor said.

"Coming up."

A chorus of "Hey, Coach" rose from Peri's patrons as Jordan made his way to the counter. He waved and clapped a couple of the younger men on the shoulder.

When he returned with steaming mugs and sat down across from Taylor, they smiled at each other, then stared in opposite directions, their conversation fading away.

ॐ

"Well, isn't Peri's the place to be?" Mia bubbled, clasping the collar of her coat around her neck, beaming up at Will as he opened her car door for her.

"Maybe it's too crowded." He hoped Taylor wouldn't be inside.

"Come on, Will. Don't be a stick-in-the-mud."

Stick-in-the-mud? He followed her, wondering how he'd gotten himself into this situation. One weak moment at Sinclair's and his night changed from a cozy evening with Grandpa and Grandma, then Harry, to an evening with frilly, silly Mia.

Lord, help. He didn't want to lead her on. He planned to make it clear they were only going to be friends.

Inside, he saw a vacant table by the door and held out a chair for Mia. "I'll get us some coffee."

"Make mine a café mocha, please."

ॐ

Taylor ran the recesses of her mind looking for a topic she thought would interest Jordan, but between the drive in the car to and from the movie, they'd exchanged all the what-are-you-up-to-now information.

Football, she thought. "The football team is doing well, I hear."

Jordan snapped to attention. "We are, so far. Eight and one."

Taylor tipped her head to the side, her eyes wide. "Good for you. Going to the play-offs then."

"Yes, then to state." Jordan made a praying gesture with his hands. "Lord willing."

"I hope you do. I know the boys on the team would be thrilled."

"You should know."

She sipped her cocoa. "Me?"

"State championship, girl's basketball. Power forward Taylor Jo Hanson."

"We lost."

"At state. Runners-up. Not too shabby. Weren't you MVP?"

"Long time ago, Jordan, in a land far, far away."

He scoffed. "You're a great athlete, Taylor. Last week's touch football game proved that."

"I love sports. Will and I used to. . ." She stopped, not meaning to mention his name.

"Is there anything between the two of you?" Jordan asked outright.

"No," Taylor said, reaching for a stir stick, swirling the whipped cream into the chocolate. "We're just friends. Well, business associates, really."

Jordan raised a brow. "Business associates?"

"I'm working with Lambert's Furniture as a consultant until I find a new job."

He nodded with an I-see look. "So you're not planning on staying in town long."

She motioned with her hand. "No, not at all. Temporary stop."

❧

Will ordered then leaned against the counter, facing Peri's small stage as the guitar player took the stool and tuned up.

Glancing around, he recognized almost everyone in the place, then his gaze connected directly with Taylor Hanson's.

He squared his shoulders as his heartbeat picked up. He gave Taylor a half smile and waved.

She half smiled and waved.

Jordan sat on the other side, his back to Will. He seemed engaged in the conversation with Taylor, though from Will's point of view, it seemed rather one-sided.

Taylor looked uncomfortable, and Will grimaced, realizing it was probably his presence that did it, not Jordan's.

Mia, on the other hand, was engaged in a lively chat with the people at the table next to theirs. She gave Will a wild wave when she caught his attention.

"Here you go, Will." Sissy Larson tapped him on the shoulder. "Two large café mochas."

"Thanks, Sissy." Will picked up the mugs and worked his way back to his table. When he sat down, he realized he was directly in Taylor's line of sight.

He ducked his head and sipped his coffee, burning his lip.

Mia propped her chin in her hand and leaned toward Will. "So, what have you been up to these days?"

"Working, mostly." He nodded. "Working."

"Oh, I love a workingman. So romantic."

Will winced with an inward sigh. It was going to be a long night.

❧

Taylor stared out the window. What was Will doing here with Mia? Were they on a date?

She picked up her hot chocolate and took a big sip, concealing most of her face with the bottom of the mug, and cut a glance across Peri's to where Will sat.

He watched the guitar player now, nodding his head to the rhythm of the song. Mia had her chin in her hand and seemed to be talking.

"More hot chocolate?" Jordan stood. "I could use another cup of coffee."

"Yes, please." *Anything for a distraction.* Jealousy tugged at her. But didn't Will have every right to be here with anyone he pleased? Especially after the speech she gave him.

While she was enjoying her time with Jordan, deep down, Taylor knew he wasn't the one. She glanced toward the counter where Jordan chatted with several men, waiting for their order. Reaching into her purse, she pulled out her electronic data assistant and jotted a note to e-mail or call Indiana Godwin again. Taylor slid the device back into her bag just as Jordan returned, with Mia clinging to his arm.

"Taylor, this is a fellow teacher and friend of mine, Mia Wilmington."

Taylor shook Mia's hand. "We've met."

"That's right. At Italian Hills. Good to see you again."

"Right." Taylor shifted her gaze beyond Mia to Will. He was looking right at her.

"Say, why don't you and Jordy join Will and me? We'd love it."

"Oh, I don't know. . ." Taylor shot Jordan what she hoped was a no-let's-not look.

"Taylor, what do you say?" Jordan asked excitedly.

Not only had he missed her visual petition, he seemed to like the idea. So the evening wasn't magical for Jordan, either.

"Okay, if you want to." She grabbed her things and stood.

"Oh, wonderful," Mia said, her arm still hooked to Jordan's as they went over to give Will the good news.

❧

Was it possible for the night to go from bad to worse? Finding himself in the company of the woman he loved while on a coffee date with a woman he didn't?

He stood as Taylor approached. "Hello."

"Hello." She gave him a slow smile.

"Isn't this cozy?" Mia said as she sat down between the men. Taylor took an awkward seat off to the side, but the fragrance of her perfume invaded Will's senses. His coffee tasted even sweeter now.

He thought to focus on the guitar player's lovely tune, lovely words. *Focus.*

"Will," Jordan started, "Taylor and I were reminiscing about the 1990 championship basketball team."

"Were you now?" Will peered into her eyes.

"Just for a moment."

Jordan continued. "Taylor doesn't think it was any big deal to go to state or be named MVP."

She lifted her hands in defense. "We lost."

"But you went to state."

Mia fluttered in her chair like a disturbed hen. "What's all this sports talk? There are ladies present."

"Sports talk is fine with me," Taylor said.

Will bit his lip to keep from laughing. Her words weren't rude or snippy. They were honest—another reason why he loved her.

Their conversation quieted down during the last song of the singer's set, and when the young man finished, the patrons applauded cordially.

Will glanced between Jordan and Taylor. "What'd you guys do tonight?"

She answered. "Went to a movie."

"Good." He was so close he could have kissed her cheek.

Mia seemed to want the conversation to be about her—or at least things she liked—so she took over. Jordan engaged her, genuinely amused.

An hour later, the foursome stood to leave.

"Well look at that, snowing again," Mia said with a giggle as she slipped on her coat. "We'll be buried before Thanksgiving at this rate."

Will thought the scene looked beautiful, and if he had his way, he'd be holding Taylor close on a moonlit walk in the fresh snow.

He turned to Mia. "Good night." He shook her hand and purposefully added, "Good to run into you at Sinclair's."

"We must do this more often. The four of us," Mia said, unlocking her car.

Mia got into her car. Will watched as Taylor left with Jordan, a gnawing of jealousy in his middle.

Taylor stopped and gazed back at him. "Good night."

twelve

The pews for the ten-thirty service were almost full by the time Taylor arrived at White Birch Community Church with her mother and dad. Tim and Dana had saved seats for them near the front.

Taylor sat on the end, grateful to be near the front and away from any distractions. If Will or Jordan were in the back, she wouldn't even know. This morning she longed to focus on Jesus and His peace.

She'd awakened this morning with the familiar feeling of hopelessness, wondering if her life would never be right again. Would she find the right job? Would she ever surrender to love?Ribbons of sunlight filtered through the sanctuary windows. Taylor closed her eyes and exhaled, the presence of the Lord already touching her heart.

Someone patted her shoulder. "Move over."

Taylor refused to open her eyes, but she recognized Will's voice. "No."

"Taylor." He gently pressed his hand on her arm.

"Good morning, Will," Grant said. "Here, sit." Taylor peeked at her dad, who was moving over to make room for Will.

"Thank you, Grant. Good morning, Trixie."

Taylor watched Will through narrowed eyes as he hugged her mom, shook hands with Tim and Dana, then shared a man-slapping hug with Pastor Marlow.

Will looked amazing in his black suit, white shirt, and sage and gold tie. Her heartbeat faltered a little when he sat down next to her and said softly, "Taylor."

"Will," she echoed.

"Have a nice Friday night?"

"Lovely," she said with a smirk. "And you?"

"Swell."

His intonation made her laugh. She covered her mouth with the tips of her fingers. She wanted to ask him how he ended up at Peri's with Mia, but the worship leader took the stage and Taylor rose to her feet with the rest of the congregation.

Jeremiah strummed his guitar. "Let's worship the Lord this morning in Spirit and truth."

A chorus of "amens" echoed around the room.

"I'm here to focus on Jesus, so don't bother me," Taylor said to Will, leaning close so only he could hear.

"I was about to say the same to you."

Grinning, she joined in the song. *Oh, Will. . . You do have a way of getting under my skin.*

❧

Will could have stayed in the sanctuary all day with Taylor. Hanging out with Jesus and Taylor. Did it get any better?

He listened closely to Pastor Marlow's sermon, making a mental note not to let Taylor's reaction to him push him toward anxiety.

Shifting his gaze for a quick second, he looked over at her. Without pondering, he knew he could love her for the rest of his life. He wanted to love her. Not only was she beautiful with her sleek nose, long eyelashes, and stubborn chin, she challenged him to be better, to look at life as an adventure, and to see people, not a list of to-dos.

Will needed Taylor. And with God's grace, he'd woo her heart.

Jesus wooed his heart every day, teaching him to respond in love. And in some small way, Will understood that the Lord loved him the way he loved Taylor.

"Let peace guard your heart and mind," Marlow concluded. "Pursue peace."

Will nodded and almost uttered amen. From the other side of the church, he heard Grandpa Matt vocalize his agreement with the message.

"Let's stand and pray." Marlow stepped from behind the pulpit.

Will stood. Next to him, Taylor rose to her feet, her expression serious.

"Everything okay?" he whispered.

She put on a bright smile. "Yes. I needed that message today."

"Words I live by." When the service ended, Will was about to ask her to lunch when Tim popped up between them.

"Do you two want to go to lunch?"

Taylor shook her head. "I had a big breakfast. I'm not really that hungry."

There went Will's idea to invite her to lunch.

"Suit yourself. Dana and I are taking Mom and Dad to the new steak place out by the theaters."

"Okay, but Dad needs to drop me home first."

Tim winced. "He already left. Mom wanted to stop by the drugstore to pick up his medication."

"Then you'll have to take me, big brother." Taylor popped him on the arm.

Will blurted, "I'll take you."

Tim grinned. "Thanks, Will. See you later, Taylor." And he was gone.

Will jerked his thumb over his shoulder. "My truck is on this side."

Taylor picked up her Bible and journal. "How convenient for you. If I didn't know better, I'd say you fixed this." She walked toward the foyer. "I need my coat."

"I'll drive around front to pick you up."

She started down the aisle. Will turned toward the side door as Grandma came up behind him. "Remember my advice now—from the other night."

Will smiled down at her. "I will."

❧

Taylor talked to herself. "Just be cool. Don't agree to anything. No dinners or walks in the park. Just thank Will for the ride home and say, 'See you tomorrow.'"

Taylor hopped inside the warm cab of Will's truck. She chuckled softly as she thought of Jordan's heat-deprived car Friday night.

"Did I miss something?" Will asked, waving to Bobby, Elle, and the kids as they passed in front of the truck.

Taylor waved, too, then said, "Jordan's car doesn't have heat. We were so cold that night."

"He's a good guy."

"He's sweet." But he wasn't Will.

Will turned south out of the church parking lot, the afternoon sun burning bright and warm through the windshield. Patches of grass showed along the road as the warm sun melted the snow.

"Beautiful day," she said without really thinking. The words simply flowed from her heart.

"You're beautiful."

She looked at him. "Stop—"

He turned onto Main. "I mean it, Taylor."

She stared ahead, letting his words sink in, allowing herself to enjoy the compliment—for a moment. Then she asked, "What about Mia?"

"I told you we're friends." Will looked over. "I ran into her at Sinclair's Friday night. She insisted I go with her to Peri's for coffee. I couldn't say no without being rude."

Taylor nodded. "I see."

As he neared the Hansons', he asked, "Are you sure you aren't hungry?"

"Well, maybe a little. I told Tim I wasn't hungry partly because I am watching my spending. I didn't want to splurge on a big lunch I don't really need."

Taylor knew when she left New York it would be tight, but she'd planned to have a job long before now. The offer from Will to work at Lambert's Furniture came just in time. She might not have to sell her new BMW.

Will pulled into the Hansons' driveway. He shifted the transmission into PARK and turned to Taylor. "How about a little basketball?"

"What? No."

"It's a beautiful day, the snow's melting, and I need a little exercise."

Taylor reached for the door handle. "No thanks."

"Win or lose, I buy lunch." Will regarded her with his deep-set blue eyes, his arm propped on the steering wheel.

"No."

He touched her arm. "One-on-one. Milo Park. Burgers at Sam's afterward."

Taylor's lips formed the word no, but her stomach lurched when she pictured one of Sam's burgers. "I don't know. . ."

"Stick-in-the-mud." He winked and laughed.

"Stick-in-the-mud?" She jerked the door open and stepped out.

"Heard it from Mia. She called me a stick-in-the-mud when I hesitated about going for coffee with her."

"I always thought more of you, Will. A little name-calling never seemed to move you before."

His gaze intent on her, he asked one more time, "Milo Park in a half hour? I need to change."

"You're on." Taylor stepped the rest of the way out of the truck and slammed the door shut.

Walking up to the house, she muttered to herself, "Right, Taylor. Say no. Just tell him thanks for the ride and see you tomorrow."

૨૮

Sam's was quiet on Sunday night, so when Taylor and Will entered, they had their pick of booth or table.

"Any one you want, Will," Sam called to him. "How are you, Taylor?"

"Fine, thank you, Sam."

Will led the way to a table by the fireplace. "I never get to sit here; these tables are always taken or reserved."

Janet came up behind them. "Evening. What would you two like to drink?"

"Diet soda and a large water for me," Taylor said, draping

her coat over the back of a chair.

"Same for me, Janet."

Taylor sat down and regarded him. His cheeks were red from playing ball, and his hair stood on end where he'd combed it with his fingers. "You were one terrible basketball player today."

He laughed. "I had lead feet this afternoon."

"Thanks for talking me into it. It was fun."

Janet set their drinks down and pulled out her order pad. "Do you know what you want?"

Will looked at Taylor and ordered for both of them. "Cheeseburgers—"

"With the works," Taylor added.

Will nodded. "And fries."

"Extra fries."

Janet lowered her pen and pad. "Are you starving, Taylor?"

"Yes."

"Anything else?" Will asked.

"Side salad for me. Light dressing on the side. No croutons."

Janet snickered as she walked away.

"Have to watch my calories," Taylor said to Will.

He shook his head, laughing with an echo of pleasure. "You amaze me, Taylor."

She fiddled with her straw wrapper. "How so?"

"You have your own way of living life. You go for your dreams. You understand God's grace—"

"But you understand His peace."

"I do. But it's been a lot of years pursing peace to be able to abide in it."

"I can't remember the last time I abided in peace."

"This morning, at church."

Tears stung her eyes. "For a moment, yes."

"Life's been difficult the past month, Taylor. Give yourself a break."

"The past month? Will, my life has been one big anxiety attack for years. Fighting to advance my career, working eighty-hour weeks. . . . Dating so-called Christian men whose morals are no different than most non-Christian men's. Worried about money. Worried about friends, worried about gray hairs and wrinkles and the world coming to an end."

Will sat back. "The world coming to an end?"

"Once I get into a worry cycle, it's hard to stop." She snickered.

"Memorizing and applying Scripture changed life for me. Grandpa and Grandma taught me about living a life of peace—about being a man of peace."

"That's what I admire about you, Will. You are so peaceful."

"I've had to work at it—change my thinking."

Janet set down Taylor's salad. Sam tossed another log on the fire. "Temperature's dropping," he said.

Taylor picked up her silverware. "I could use a few lessons."

"I could teach you. Pray with you."

She smiled. "I'd rather not, Will."

"Why not?" He couldn't let her comment go.

She looked him square in the eye. "You know why."

"Tell me."

She sighed, her fork loose in her hand. "I'll fall in love with you."

"Then we're even."

thirteen

By Friday noon, Taylor and Markie had mapped out their work flow and created a project plan that started with the day they purchased the new system to "go live."

Happy with the plan and the demo HBS gave them earlier in the week, Taylor recommended Lambert's Furniture purchase HBS for their accounting, timekeeping, and inventory system.

"Knock, knock." Will smiled and held up the papers in his hand. Harry followed, his tail wagging.

"Come in." She returned his smile, remembering her Monday morning promise to lighten up with Will yet maintain a safe distance. She had concluded that playing the gruff, once-rejected woman didn't fit her character or God's.

But it took until Thursday evening to stop daydreaming about their Sunday afternoon basketball game and eating burgers afterward at Sam's in front of the fire.

They'd had a great time that day. Being in Will's company always felt like coming home at the end of a hard day: peaceful, warm, and sheltered.

She drew a deep breath. "Did you sign the HBS deal?"

Will walked over to the fireplace and turned on the gas. "It's always colder on this side of the building." Harry sniffed Taylor's leg then passed by to curl up by the stone hearth.

"That's why I wear a parka and drink ten cups of coffee."

He laughed and handed her a copy of the contract. "You are an excellent negotiator. The salesman couldn't stop telling us how amazing you were."

"Let's see if he put in my last request for changes to the terms and conditions." She skimmed the contract down to the fine print. "Yep, he did."

"If you wanted a job with HBS, Taylor, you could probably get one."

She snapped her head up. "What?"

"He asked about you. I told him that you were only consulting."

"Thank you, but I know some things about HBS internally. Not my cup of tea. They make a great product, but I wouldn't want to be on the inside."

He nodded.

"Thank you, anyway, again." She looked down when their eyes met.

"You're welcome," Will said then left.

Taking her wide desk chair, Taylor felt disappointed with the simple, straightforward business conversation she'd just had with Will. Was she crazy or did she really want him to pursue her? Never mind her continuous song of "I'm not available"?

Her phone rang just as she reaffirmed, again, that falling in love with Will did not fit her agenda.

"Taylor, it's Indiana."

She smiled. "I was going to call you."

"I have a job lead for you."

She stood, shooting her chair across the hardwood floor. "Really? Where? What?"

"Boswell Global in Sacramento is looking for a CFO."

"You're kidding." Boswell Global was a hot new dot-com company.

"A friend, Alex Cranston, is their human resource director. We were talking, and he wanted to know if I knew any qualified financial officer candidates."

Taylor sank toward her seat, which she realized wasn't there, so she perched on the edge of the desk. "Did you tell him about me?"

"I did. They're looking for young, chic, savvy executives. You're perfect for the job."

"Indiana, that's incredible," Taylor said. She asked several questions about the position, jotted down Alex Cranston's e-mail address, and thanked Indiana one last time.

"I wouldn't recommend you if I didn't think you were qualified, Taylor."

They talked a few more minutes about old job acquaintances and then said good-bye. Taylor felt as if she were flying. She balled her fist and allowed herself one controlled squeal.

By the hearth, Harry lifted his head and whined.

"I'm fine, Harry," she said, her hand pressed to her forehead. "Lord, I can't believe You answered my prayer with Boswell Global."

Without wasting any more time, Taylor launched her e-mail program and composed a warm, but brief letter to Alex Cranston and attached her résumé.

California, get ready to meet Taylor Hanson.

&

At Peri's, Will ordered and took a stool at one of the high, round tables. He waved when his grandparents came in holding hands. "What are you young people doing?"

Grandma laughed. "Having lunch. Your grandpa is addicted to Peri's sweet coffees."

Grandpa shook Will's hand. "Hardly fair to call it coffee with so much whipped cream floating on top."

Will nodded in agreement. "How are things down in the shop?"

"Good. But I'm looking forward to Grant's return. I retired for a reason, you know."

Will shook his head. "You volunteered."

"I did. And I've enjoyed it." Grandpa held Grandma's chair for her. "But I'm ready to be home with your grandma again and puttering around the basement, working on my own projects."

"Ethan said Grant will be back after Thanksgiving."

Grandpa nodded. "He deserves some time off."

Grandma tapped Will on the hand. "What's going on with you?"

Will sat in the spare seat across from his grandparents. "We just signed a deal with Hayes Business Systems. Couldn't have done it without Taylor."

"What does that mean for the business?" Grandma asked.

Will grinned. "It's a major software upgrade. We launch our e-business as soon as the installation is done and live. Selling furniture over the Internet. . .did you ever imagine that, Grandpa?"

Grandpa shook his head. "No, but the Lord is really blessing the business, isn't He?"

Will nodded. "He amazes me every day. The fact Taylor was available with the talent and experience we needed is a miracle."

Grandma tapped his hand. "What is going on with you two? Elizabeth and Kavan drove by the park Sunday afternoon and saw you two playing basketball."

Will laughed. "My cousin, Elizabeth, the romance reporter. Remember when she met Kavan and practically despised falling in love?"

"She's a changed woman," Grandma said with a low laugh. "So, how goes the plan to win Taylor? Did you let her beat you in basketball?"

"I'm executing it one day at a time, just like you told me."

"Will, your order's up," Peri called.

Grandma pointed at him. "Don't let her go this time."

Will frowned as he stepped over to the counter and picked up his grilled chicken sandwich. "I'll try not to, Grandma. But she has her own plans."

"What's next on the wooing Taylor agenda?" Grandma asked as he took his seat.

Will shrugged. "What should it be?"

Grandma's expression told him it should be obvious. "Flowers."

❧

At four o'clock Will walked into Taylor's office. He gently grabbed her arm and lifted her from her chair.

"Come on," he said, guiding her toward the door.

"Will, wait. I'm in the middle of something. Where are we going?"

"It's Friday afternoon. Time to cut out for some fun."

"I'm having fun working. Markie and I came up with a great plan to move the data from the old system."

"Good. But it's quitting time." He tugged on her arm again. "You want to tell me what's up?"

He grinned. "Football."

She headed back to her desk. "Oh, no. Not me."

"Lambert's Furniture needs you." He bent over her, hands pressed on the arms of her chair. "Ethan challenged Creager Technologies in a touch game, and we can't lose."

"Will, I have work to do." She'd calculated the time it would take to get the office ready for a new system, then change over from the old one, and she needed several more weeks of intense effort. If Boswell hired her, she didn't want to leave Lambert's in a bind.

Besides, spending her free time with Will was dangerous to her heart.

"It's Friday at four, Taylor. Stop and smell the roses."

"I, um, just don't want to. . ." He moved a little closer. She cleared her throat and looked away. ". . .to fall behind."

"Next week you can work to your heart's content. But for now, play football with us. The company needs you."

Grrr. He was hard to resist. "I thought Sunday was football day."

"This is a special game. We have a little friendly sporting rivalry going with the engineering firm." He reached for her purse and took her hand. "Come on, Taylor. Think of your Lambert's Furniture coworkers." He furrowed his brow, apparently attempting to look pitiful.

She broke. "Fine, but that's the worst pity face I've ever seen."

"I'm new at this."

She slipped her hand from his and walked with him to the door. "But this is the last time, Will."

He stopped and faced her. "Why does this have to be the last time?"

She gathered her fortitude, stepped into his personal space, and said, "Because you are dangerous, and I'm not putting my heart on the line."

He didn't hesitate. "Well, I am."

Her heart stopped beating for a second. What? She gathered herself and quipped, "I wouldn't if I were you. The lifeguard isn't on duty."

"I can swim."

Will was dead serious, and it petrified her. She took her purse from him and headed down the hall. "Give me twenty minutes to go home and change."

"See you at the park."

&

Taylor hurried through the kitchen and up the back staircase to her room.

"Taylor?" her mother called up the stairs. "It's been a busy day around here for you."

"Me?" she asked, poking her head around the door.

"Yes, you. Come down."

"I'm playing football in the park. I need to change and get over there."

"Oh, Taylor, again? You're thirty-three. When are you going to start acting like a lady?"

Taylor laughed and looked down the stairs at her mother. "When it becomes as much fun to be a *lady* as it is to play football."

Mom's willowy hand muffled her dainty chortle. "Come down."

"In a minute." Taylor changed quickly for football, leaving her jeans and oxford shirt on the floor, her thoughts fractured between a job opportunity thousands of miles away and a handsome quarterback in a little flag football game two miles away.

Taylor bounded down the stairs. "Okay, what's up?"

"Didn't you see?" Mom asked.

"See what?" Taylor glanced at her mother's piquant face.

"Flowers." Mom motioned to the dining room table.

Taylor walked to the adjoining room where she found the most beautiful bouquet of red roses she'd ever seen. She reached for the card.

Taylor, for the night I should have said yes.

Love,
Will

She trembled as a geyser of emotions erupted from deep within. What? Will, no!

Her eyes burned and her jaw tightened. Deep breaths held back the tears. She wouldn't let go.

"Who are they from, Taylor?" Mom called from the family room.

"Will."

"Will?"

"Yes, Mom." She cleared the emotion from her voice. "Didn't you say something about it being the day of Taylor? Did something else come for me?"

Mom came around the corner. "You had a phone call from an Alex Cranston. I believe he said he was calling from California." She handed Taylor a piece of paper.

Taylor read Alex Cranston's name and number written carefully in her mother's perfect handwriting. Her heart raced. "Did he say anything else?"

"He asked if you could call as soon as possible."

Taylor forced a smile as she folded the note in her hand. "I'll call him on my cell." She snatched up her car keys, the vase of roses, and the note with Alex Cranston's number. "I'll be back later."

fourteen

Will watched her stride across the field. It didn't seem right to him that a woman should look so beautiful and graceful wearing dingy old sweats.

She stopped when she got to him. "Can I see you? Over here?" She motioned toward the cars.

"Hello, Taylor." Jordan jogged up to her private huddle with Will.

"Hi, Jordan." She gave him a slight hug. "Are you playing today?"

He grinned. "Drafted by Creager."

She lifted her chin. "I see." Looking around him, she scanned the opposing team. "Will, isn't that your cousin Jeff?"

Will nodded. "My cousin Elizabeth used to work at Creager. She drafted Jeff and her husband, Kavan, for their teams." He pointed to a redheaded man standing next to Jeff.

"Family against family? Should be interesting." Then she turned to Jordan. "Will you excuse us?"

"Sure."

She smiled and patted him on the arm. "Thanks." Taylor turned to Will and motioned for him to follow her.

"What's up?" he asked, leaning in close when they stopped beside her car. His heart was smiling. Surely she saw the roses when she went home.

She opened the passenger door, reached in, and pulled out the flowers. "I can't accept these." She shoved the vase at Will.

His heart sank, but he kept his expression the same. "Why not?"

"Because I can't. We can't undo the last ten years."

"No, but we can start over."

She shoved the flowers at him again. "My actions that night

were a foolish romantic notion. Let's not revisit it, shall we?"

"I'm not taking the roses back, Taylor." He stood with his feet apart, his arms crossed over his chest, one hand gripping the football.

"I'm not accepting them." She set the flowers on the ground and met his gaze, then placed her hands on her hips.

He reacted. He pulled Taylor to him and kissed her. She pushed away at first then melted into his embrace.

When he lifted his head, she muttered, "I wish you'd stop doing that."

He pressed his forehead to hers. "I guess it's not the best way to communicate."

"What are you trying to say?"

"I love you."

She drew a shaky breath. "Then you definitely have to stop."

He hooked his finger under her chin and lifted her head. Looking into her eyes, he said, "Give us a chance."

She gripped his forearms. "Now is not the time, Will."

"It's the perfect time."

Someone called from the field. "Hey, are you two going to play ball or kiss? We're losing daylight."

"The timing isn't perfect," she said as she walked backward toward the field and away from him.

He ducked his head, pressing his hand on the back of his neck, thinking. How should he respond to her determination? With more determination?

As he jogged back to the field, he clung to the peace he harbored in his heart and Grandma's advice. *Let her know I love her. Don't give up.*

&

"If you move to California, I don't know what we'll do without you, Taylor," Mom said Saturday. She sat on the edge of the ottoman in the family room, her back straight, sewing squares together for a quilt.

"Same as you always did, Mom," Taylor said, waiting for Dad to move a rook or pawn. "Dad, are you going to make a move?"

He glanced up from the chessboard. "You cannot rush genius."

Taylor laughed and relaxed against the back of her chair. "I've been wanting a job like this one for a long time. I can't believe I'm even getting a shot at Boswell Global."

"California is so far away," Mom lamented.

"I'll come home on vacations. You all can visit me in California. It'll be great."

The phone rang. Taylor volunteered to answer since her dad was still contemplating his move and Mom had blocks of material on her lap.

"Taylor, it's Jordan."

"Hey." She moved to the living room with the cordless. The fragrance of Will's roses wafted in from the dining room. He'd refused to take them back, so Taylor brought them home with her.

"I enjoyed our date the other night."

"It was a nice night. But, Jordan, I—"

"I ran into Mia again," he interrupted, "and we started talking, and well, we've had dinner together every night this week."

Taylor bit her lips, trying not to laugh. Jordan and Mia? They were perfect for each other. "That's great."

"It looks like you and Will still have a thing for each other anyway."

"No," she protested. "No, we are just friends."

Jordan snorted. "I saw that kiss, Taylor. Will's mind is made up."

"It doesn't matter what Will wants."

Jordan chuckled. "Did you tell him that?"

Taylor sat on the sofa, a Lambert's Furniture classic piece. "As a matter of fact, I did. Besides, I have a job opportunity in California."

"Really? Then go for it, if that's what you want."

Taylor pressed her hand over her eyes. "It's what I want."

"Keep me posted."

"I will. Good luck with Mia."

"I'll send you a wedding invitation."

She made a face at the phone. "You think it will come to that?"

"I think so." They talked for a few more minutes and exchanged e-mail addresses.

When she hung up and replaced the phone on the cradle, Tim, Dana, and the kids walked through the door.

"The boys thought Grandpa needed an ice cream sundae," Tim said, unloading ice cream, whipped cream, several sauces, peanuts, chocolate, and cherries.

"Wow," Taylor said, hugging her nephews, praising them for their choice of desserts. Mom hurried about the kitchen, setting bowls and spoons on the counter.

Claire put on a CD, and the quiet house came alive with the melodies of a family.

Dad, however, remained poised over his chess pieces, calculating his next move. Laughing, Taylor coaxed him from his chair.

"You can't keep company with the chessboard when your grandsons were kind enough to bring over ice cream."

He stretched and patted his belly. "I guess ice cream would hit the spot." He high-fived his grandsons. "You boys always did know how to treat your old pop."

Taylor watched, her heart beating to the rhythm of the family's voices and laughter. *This,* she thought, *this I will miss.*

A half hour later, Tim sat in Taylor's chair opposing Dad in chess, who had yet to make his genius move.

Quentin and Jarred watched a movie in the living room, and Taylor sat at the dining table with Mom, Dana, and Claire.

Taylor realized for the first time in a long time, anxiety wasn't wheedling her into worrying. She felt the Lord's assurance. He would work out the details of her life.

"Okay, I can't take it anymore," Dana said. "Where did you get these roses, Mom? They are beautiful." She stood and leaned toward the bouquet, sniffing. "So fragrant."

"Will sent them to Taylor."

Claire's mouth dropped open. She grabbed Taylor's arm. "Oh, wow. Are you in love or what?"

"No, I'm not in love."

"Oh, Taylor, please," Dana said. "You and Will Adams are meant for each other."

"What? How so?"

The women talked at once. "You're perfect for each other."

"He's quiet, you're loud."

"I am not loud," Taylor protested.

"You both love sports. You both love the Lord."

"You're best friends."

Finally, Taylor stopped them. "Fine," Taylor said with a slap of her hand on the table. "But we are not getting together. Period."

Dana laughed and pointed at her sister-in-law. "I'll be singing at your wedding before this time next year."

Taylor spread her arms and chimed, "Wonderful. I'd love that, but Will won't be the groom."

"We'll see," said Dana. "We'll see."

&

Wednesday afternoon Will sat in the conference room with Bobby, Markie, and Taylor reviewing the HBS installation schedule.

"It's tight. We have a lot to get done in eight weeks." Will looked up from Taylor's project plan.

"With year-end coming up," Taylor started, "I recommend converting over to HBS in January. Start the new fiscal year on the new system. Only transfer the data you need and keep the old system in maintenance mode."

"We still have to move account and billing records forward," Markie said. "But I'm eager to get the staff trained."

"I need to get the sales team in here for training on the contact management system," Bobby said.

Taylor smiled. "They'll love it. It will increase their sales."

"That's what I want to hear." Bobby slapped his hands on the table.

Taylor motioned to Markie. "You need to get a data dump from the old system so HBS can get to work on the conversion program. We can't do anything without the account records and inventory data."

Markie nodded, typing on her computer. "Will, I might need your help with that," she said.

"No problem."

After the meeting, Taylor stopped Will outside his office door. "Can I talk to you?"

"Sure." He stepped aside for her to enter his office. Things had been distant and cool between them since his impetuous kiss on the football field. He apologized Sunday after church and kept his distance in the office.

While he hated the strain between them, Will planned to relentlessly pursue her.

"What can I do for you?" He motioned to the chair by his desk, but she remained standing.

Hands clasped in front of her, she looked at him, her gaze seeming unfocused. "I have a job interview next week in California. I leave Monday, fly back Wednesday."

Will kicked out his chair and sat. "I see." This news definitely put a kink in his plan.

"It's an amazing company, Boswell Global. They are an emerging dot-com. They need a new CFO."

"You don't have to convince me." He picked up a short blue pen lying on his desk and began clicking it, on and off, on and off.

She bristled. "I'm not convincing you. I just wanted to let you know."

"Taylor, if this opportunity means so much to you, then—" He jammed the pen into a holder.

"It does. But I wanted you to know I will finish what I started here."

"If you have to go, then you have to go. We didn't contract you for any length of time." His hands gripped the arms of his chair.

She narrowed her gaze. "I don't want to abandon the job."

"Look, we got a great deal on the business system, thanks to you. Markie has the project plan. I run a multimillion dollar company; I think I can manage the installation."

She bristled. "Of course, I didn't meant to imply you couldn't handle the install, Will. But you contracted me for my expertise and. . ."

She was fishing, Will decided. If she chose not to go to California, she'd have to come up with a better reason than the new business system.

She stared down into the manufacturing plant. "I'll probably wait until after Christmas to move."

"If you get the job."

She snapped her head around. "Yes, if I get the job."

He walked over to her. "It'd be great to have you around for the holidays."

She stared again at the crew below. "I haven't been around for many holidays lately. Claire and the boys are getting older. Daddy's scare made me think how much family time I've missed. I'd really like to be home for this Christmas."

"You don't have to convince me."

She whipped around. "I'm not trying to convince you. I'm just saying. . ." She sat in the vacant chair. "What do you think?"

"About what?"

She stared at her hands and asked softly, "About the job. About me moving to California."

He slipped his hands in his pockets and peered into her face. "You always get what you want."

She stared straight into his eyes. "Not always."

"Now's your chance."

fifteen

Sunday evening Taylor packed an overnight tote and zipped her best suit into a garment bag.

"What do you think, Mom, taupe or black pumps?" Taylor walked into her parents' room with a sample of each pair.

Mom didn't look up from the chaise lounge where she sat with her sewing. "What color is your suit?"

"Dark red."

"Pants or skirt?"

"Skirt."

Mom set her sewing aside and motioned to see the shoes. "Black," she said after a short inspection.

"Really? I like the taupe." Taylor examined the shoes under the light. Who was she to question the impeccable Trixie Hanson? She'd wear the black.

"Are you sure this move is right for you, Taylor?" Mom asked, picking up her quilting pieces again.

"Y—yes." Her answer didn't sound as confident as she wanted. "How can I turn such an opportunity down?"

From the library, Taylor heard the rustle of her father's newspaper. He came through the door a second later.

"Well, how much does the opportunity cost?" He settled on the chaise with Mom.

Taylor sat on the edge of the bed, dropping the shoes to the floor. "What do you mean?"

Dad examined a square of gingham. "If you want this position, you go to California and win it. Let Boswell see the excellent abilities of Taylor Jo Hanson. But think about what it will cost you in time and relationships."

She regarded him, half of her bare foot in the taupe pump. "I've calculated the cost, Dad." She slipped her foot the rest of the way into the shoe. She did like them better.

"Mom, I'm going with the taupe." She shoved her other foot into the black pump and stood.

"Your choice, Taylor."

"I don't think you have, Taylor," Dad said, firm and low. "Don't go to California if there is the remotest chance that you are in love with Will."

Taylor whirled around. "In love with him? He's a friend, period."

She walked toward the floor-length mirror to check out the shoes.

Oh, pain. She kicked off both shoes, remembering now why the soles were barely worn on the taupe pair. They pinched her toes.

"I'm wearing the black." She picked up her shoes, grimacing at the taupe.

Trixie laughed softly. "I had a pair of taupe shoes that hurt my feet, too. But I loved them."

"Taylor," Dad said as she started to leave.

"What, Daddy?" She held up the black pump. "Maybe I should wear my beige suit."

Mom glanced up. "No, it will make you look too pale. Let me look at your wardrobe."

Trixie went past Taylor into her bedroom.

Dad finished his thought. "You won't get another chance at Will. So, pray about it long and hard."

Heat picked its way across her cheeks and down her neck. "I hear you, but I don't think it changes anything."

He came over to her and rested his hand on her arm. "I've watched you over the years, Taylor. There's more to the story than you're telling your mom and me."

She stared at the floor. "It's over. Forgotten."

"You left town like your hair was on fire. And if I remember right, you were in love with him."

"Correct. Were—was."

"You're a grown woman, Taylor, and I've seen you make

some excellent decisions. Make sure this California job is the Lord's leading, not you running away from the ghost of summers past."

She lifted her head and jutted out her chin. "I am praying, Dad."

"All right. Just know that if you move to California, Will won't be single and waiting when you come home again."

She jutted out her chin. "So you've said."

Dad embraced her. "I love you, and I would like nothing more than for the Lord to bless you with a godly husband."

Taylor batted away tears. "Me, too. Better see what Mom's picking out."

In her room, Mom coordinated the perfect suit and shoes. Taylor stood back, shaking her head. "Perfect. How come you didn't pass your gift of style to me, Mom?"

"I did."

"Right. I wouldn't have thought to put that rose-colored jacket with those chocolate slacks."

"You have style, Taylor. It shows in the way you wear your hair and the way you carry yourself. It shows in the way you do your job and live life. I wish I had your gusto."

"Gusto?" Taylor repeated. That was not a Trixie Hanson word.

She tossed the black and taupe pumps in the closet and pulled out a brown pair of Mary Janes.

"Yes, gusto." Mom smiled at her. "Oh, those shoes will go nicely."

"They're comfortable, too."

"When I was your age," Mom reminisced, sitting on the edge of Taylor's bed, "I sewed and crocheted and decorated cakes for church auctions. I wore hats and white gloves to social events."

Taylor sat on the edge of her desk. "Times have changed."

"Yes, they have." Mom stood, smiling. "I don't know if I'd do as well in your generation, Taylor. But I'm very proud of you."

"Don't sell yourself short, Mom. Dad told me how you stood

up to Grandpa when you and Dad wanted to get married."

"That was so long ago. I was young and in love."

Taylor regarded her. "There's no force in the world more powerful than a loved woman."

Mom stood. "No, I imagine there isn't."

After Mom went back to quilting, Taylor puttered around her room, reorganizing her overnight tote, selecting toiletries, and wondering if she should bother with her laptop.

By eight o'clock, she'd wandered restlessly through the house. She picked at the last piece of cake, split an apple with her dad, and flipped through the TV channels.

Something bugged her, deep down. She glanced at her dad. It was his words reverberating in her heart. *"You won't get another chance."*

She grabbed her car keys and called upstairs, "I'm going for a drive." She drove slowly down Main Street, passing Sam's and Earth-n-Treasures, the library, and Golda's Golden Beauty Parlor. She ran her fingers through her hair, thinking she should have gotten it cut before flying to California. But she'd doubted Golda could match the color and style of her favorite New York salon.

"If I get this job, I'm treating myself to a spa day."

On impulse she reached for her phone and autodialed Reneé but got her voice mail. "Hey, it's me. I'm leaving tomorrow for the California interview. Pray. Call you later."

She pressed END and tossed the phone into the passenger seat as the White Birch covered bridge came into view. Slowly, Taylor pulled alongside the road and parked.

There was no moon. The only light came from a street lamp and the distant glow from Grandma Betty and Grandpa Matt's home up on the hill.

Taylor pulled on her coat, zipped it all the way up, and tucked her hands into her pockets.

Walking toward the middle of the bridge, she remembered the last time she was here with Will. With love.

"Lord, is Dad right? Am I fooling myself about Will?"

She prayed, listening to the gurgle of the river and waiting on the Lord.

☙

In the basement, Will helped Grandpa put the finishing touches on a chest of drawers he was making for baby Matt.

"I'm going to want this design for the business, you know," Will said, running his hand along the polished cherrywood.

"Can't. It's special for little Matt."

"We can name it after him." Will stood back to take in the whole piece. Grandpa's designs amazed him.

The elder Lambert stood next to his grandson, his shoulders squared. "Well, maybe we can make a few changes so it's not an exact replica."

Will laughed. "Done."

He stepped over to the sink to wash up just as Grandma called down the stairs, "Hot chocolate and hot cookies in the kitchen."

Will dried his hands and said to Grandpa, "See you. I'm going up."

Grandpa waved. "I see you've got your priorities straight. I'll be up as soon as I put the tools away."

In the warm kitchen, Will sat at the breakfast nook. Harry left his warm spot by the oven to rest his chin on Will's knee.

"Only one cookie, boy, and don't tell Grandma."

"Too late; she already heard." Grandma came in with a fresh batch of dish towels. "I gave him one, too."

Will scratched Harry's ears. "He's hard to resist."

Grandma brought over two mugs of cocoa and joined Will at the table. "How goes the war of love with Taylor?"

Will set down the cookie he was about to bite into and shook his head. "She's going to California for a big job interview."

"I guess you have your work cut out for you."

"You know she tried to give me back the roses, but I refused to take them."

"You broke her heart, Will. She's not going to let you back in easily."

"What about my heart? It could get broken in this process."

"Then you'll know you gave love a chance."

"And bleed all over the place?"

"If necessary."

Grandpa came into the kitchen, shutting the basement door behind him. He sat next to Grandma and reached for a cookie.

"People today," Grandma said, getting up to pour Grandpa a mug of hot chocolate, "want love to be easy—to be fair. Fifty-fifty. But love requires you to give one hundred percent. It's not always easy, and it's not always fair."

"I'm willing to give it one hundred percent if she is."

"What if she's not? Are you going to give up? Sometimes love is about one giving a hundred percent and the other giving nothing." Grandma returned to the nook with a big, steaming mug and set it before Grandpa.

"Thank you, Betty."

Will shrugged. "I'm not sure I want to give myself to something that may end up causing pain."

"Jesus did," Grandma said.

Grandpa added, "He went to the cross, rejected by His own people, abandoned by His friends, and knowing that many more generations would also reject Him. He gave one hundred percent while we gave zero."

Will pondered that truth for a moment. What kind of love moved God to send His Son to pay the price for man's sins? What kind of love endured the brutality and rejection of the cross?

Just the thought made Will tremble inside. That same God knew and loved him.

"It moves me to humility," he said.

"If God did not spare His own Son, how will He not freely give us all things? We can trust Him," Grandpa said.

Will shook his head. "I'm amazed every time I think about what He did for us, for me."

"Will," Grandma said gently, "if you pursue Taylor and she moves away, then you'll know it wasn't meant to be. But don't give up too soon. If you ask me, whatever happened between the two of you all those years ago is still happening."

"It is, Grandma. Only we've switched places this time." Harry scratched at the door. Will stood, picking up his hot chocolate. "I'll let him out." Will reached for the knob. "There ya go, boy." Harry woofed and darted down the hill toward the bridge. Laughing, Will decided to follow. "Heeellloooo," Will shouted, running onto the bridge after Harry, the bright light of the moon lighting the way. Harry's bark echoed in the rafters. A shrill scream answered him from the other end of the bridge. "Who's there?" someone asked.

"Will Adams. Who are you?"

"You scared me, Will."

He grinned as Taylor stepped toward him. He could barely see her face in the slivers of light that reflected off the river and up through the bridge's beams. But her voice and her fragrance were undeniable.

He recognized love. "What are you doing here?" he asked as she drew closer.

She shrugged. "I went for a drive. Sitting around the house waiting for tomorrow morning was making me crazy."

"I can imagine."

She sniffed. "Hot chocolate. Hmm. . ."

"Would you like some? Grandma made a huge pot."

She stepped back, waving her hands. "No, no, I don't want to trouble Grandma Betty."

"Are you kidding me? She lives for moments like this."

"It does smell good."

He had an idea. "Don't go anywhere. I'll be right back." He set his mug down on the bridge floor and darted away. "Harry, stay here with Taylor."

"Will, wait. Will?"

He ran up the hill and into the Lambert kitchen.

Opening and closing cabinets, he searched until he found Grandpa's old fishing thermos then filled it with hot chocolate. He found a paper bag, snapped it open, and stuffed it with warm cookies.

"Should I ask what you're doing running around my kitchen like a crazed man or just not worry about it?" Grandma asked.

Will grabbed a mug. "Be at peace, Grandma." With that, he disappeared out the door.

His grandparents' muted laughter followed.

On the bridge, Taylor stood exactly where he'd left her. "Hot chocolate and cookies." He held up the bag and mug.

"Oh, wow, they smell so good."

"Where should we sit?" Will strode to the edge of the bridge. "The ground is wet."

"My car," Taylor suggested. "We can put the top down."

"Can Harry join us?"

Taylor reached to scratch the sheepdog's ears. "Of course."

With a click of a few buttons, Taylor tucked the BMW's top away. They climbed in and settled on top of the backseat. Will poured her a mug of hot chocolate and refreshed his.

"Have a cookie." He held out the bag for Taylor.

She took a bite. "Yum. These are so good."

Harry set his chin on her knee, his tail swishing against the leather seat.

"I think Harry likes you," Will said, reaching for a cookie.

Taylor giggled. "Only because I have cookies."

Will grinned. This was good, right. Only the Lord could have arranged this. "No, Harry just knows a loving woman when he meets one."

Taylor broke off a piece of her cookie and gave it to Harry. "Mom and I were talking tonight about how different women are today than when she was growing up and how different her world was from mine."

"It is amazing, isn't it?"

"She gave birth to me at thirty-three. I'm a single career woman, possibly about to land the job of a lifetime."

Will sipped from his mug. "It's what you want?"

She looked up at his face. "Yes, it's what I want."

sixteen

Taylor refilled her hot chocolate from the thermos and cupped her hands around the ceramic mug for warmth.

As much as she determined she wouldn't fall in love with Will again, she loved being in his presence. But his countenance challenged the walls around her heart, and she wondered if she would ever find another man like him.

"Favorite color?" he asked suddenly.

She laughed. "Okay. That came out of nowhere."

"Fess up; it's black isn't it?"

"Black? Not a color, my friend. Actually, I like blue."

"Favorite gem?"

"Diamonds are a girl's best friend."

"Guess I walked into that one."

"Yep." Taylor sipped her hot chocolate.

"Favorite song?"

"Now that's a hard one." Taylor thought for a moment. "I know this is corny, but I really love 'The Old Rugged Cross.'"

"I like 'Just As I Am.'"

Taylor smiled. "Both of those songs make me cry."

Harry shifted in the seat between them, curling up against the cold leather, his snout on Taylor's foot.

"You just might have to take Harry home with you," Will said, reaching down to smooth the fur on Harry's back.

"Right. That would go over real well with Trixie No-More-Pets Hanson."

Will laughed softly. "Remember when you wanted to keep that stray cat?"

Taylor nodded then sipped the last of her hot chocolate. "Talk about a cat fight."

"Okay, favorite memory?"

The question struck a chord in the resonant places of her heart. The answer was easy: Will. But she wouldn't confess it out loud. Her time with him eclipsed all the fun days of high school and college, her first apartment, and her first career job and move to New York City. It was as if life without Will had never existed.

But she had to answer with something. "Hmm, let's see." She thought about the night on the bridge. Funny, her best memory was also her worst. She decided to bail. "You go first. What's your favorite memory?"

He looked over at her then down at his empty mug. She couldn't see his face, only the outline of his symmetrical nose and chin.

"You."

A prickly sensation ran over her skin. "Me? What do you—"

"You're my favorite memory." He lifted his head, looking out into the darkness. "Playing basketball, football; eating ice cream; movie night in Franklin Murphy's basement with those of us who came home from college; driving down Old Town Road in my Camaro. . ."

Will had held her hand for the first time while driving down Old Town Road. A tingle ran across her hand as she remembered, just like it did that night.

They certainly had a strange relationship. One or two hand-holdings. One kiss. One marriage proposal. Ten years of silence.

She knew he was looking at her. "The job in California means a lot to me, Will."

"I know. I guess I wish I mattered as much."

"I'm sorry. But I've invested ten years in my career."

"Ten years that should've been with me," Will said.

"But they weren't, were they?" she answered without malice.

They were silent for a few moments. Taylor imagined it was getting late, but she didn't want to leave just yet. Tonight may be her last with Will.

"You never told me your favorite memory," Will said, reaching down for the thermos.

"I don't know if I can pick one. Maybe my first job. Oh, my first big paycheck. The year I made the cheerleader squad."

Will tipped up the thermos. A few drops flowed out into his cup. "Didn't you try out as a joke?"

Taylor laughed. "Yes, I did."

"You beat out Tammy Carter her senior year."

"Oh, that's right. Okay, that's not a favorite memory, then. I hated that I took Tammy's spot."

For a long while, they talked about high school and college, comparing experiences and tales. For a man who had lived most of his life in White Birch, Will understood a lot about the world.

Finally, he said, "I hear it never rains in California."

She laughed and bumped him with her shoulder.

Will bumped her back and scooted a little closer. Harry growled softly when Will's foot moved him into a different position.

Taylor clicked her nails against the side of her mug. "It will be a change, for sure." Why did she feel like he was going to kiss her? Did she want him to kiss her?

One last kiss. . .a kiss good-bye?

Will reached down for the empty bag of cookies. "It's late. I should get going." He pressed the backlight on his wristwatch. "Wow, it's ten thirty."

He hopped out the side of the car, and Taylor felt oddly alone.

"Do you want to put the top up?" Will asked.

She slid out of the car on the opposite side. "I'll freeze if I don't."

Will opened the passenger door and called for Harry. Taylor leaned over the wheel, turned the key in the ignition, and powered up the top.

Will walked around to the driver's side. "Have a good trip. I'll pray for you." He took her hand and pulled her into his embrace.

A shiver ran over her scalp and down her spine. She closed her eyes, waiting for his lips to touch hers.

He wrapped her in his arms, and with a light squeeze he

said, "See you in a few days. Come on, Harry."

She swallowed and muttered, her heat beating with the force of eagles' wings, "Um, yes, a few days."

❧

Boswell Global rolled out the red carpet for Taylor. Alex Cranston personally met her at the airport then escorted her around the plant as if she were the queen of England.

The early morning interviews went well, and by the time Alex met her for lunch, she wondered if she glowed.

"I see you've had a good morning," Alex said, leading her toward the parking lot and his car. "I thought we'd eat at a great little pizza place in Redwood City."

Taylor lifted her face to the warm California sun. Yesterday, New Hampshire's gray sky threatened snow. "Perfect."

Soon they were sitting on the patio under the pizza parlor's pavilion. When the waiter left with their order, Alex said, "The VP of marketing wanted to know which rainbow I followed to find you."

"Really?" Taylor sat back, lifting her chin a little. In light of her recent failure at Blankenship & Burns, it felt good to hear she'd impressed the Boswell executives.

"We have a few more candidates to interview, but my guess is you're their choice."

A spark of excitement ignited in Taylor. "I would be honored to join the Boswell Global team."

Alex asked a few typical interview questions, such as how she saw herself fitting in at the company, and, just as she expected, to describe her greatest strength and weakness.

She smiled and answered with honesty. "Ambition. Both my strength and my weakness."

Alex motioned to the waiter to refill their water glasses. "I thought so. Best weakness to have if you learn to manage it."

"Believe me, after two years on my old job, and by the grace of God, I learned to manage my ambition."

Alex regarded her after that comment but didn't probe further. "Tell me your career plans. What's up with Taylor

Hanson in five years?"

"Well," she started, prepared for this answer. In Charlotte, she'd gone over the top with her response. A month later, her perspective on life was more realistic. "I want to contribute to Boswell's vision, be a part of the decision-making process that leads us into the next generation. I'm thirty-three, so I have a lot of years ahead of me. I'm not married, so I can be devoted to the company."

"Good to hear," Alex said, smiling and reaching for his water. "Off the record, it's a plus that you're not married for now."

"How so?"

"The last CFO left us in a little bit of a mess. You're going to have your job cut out for you."

"I see." Taylor absorbed the reality of what Alex communicated. He set his water down. "Don't worry; the pay is worth it."

She smiled. "Good to know."

Their pizza arrived, and the conversation went to more casual topics, such as the surrounding communities and life in northern California.

Yet thoughts of Will interrupted her concentration. She shifted in her chair and focused on eating a slice of pizza, shoving images of Will back to New Hampshire.

"Boswell seems to have a strong team environment," Taylor finally said. "I like that."

A lot like Lambert's Furniture, she thought. She answered that with an internal *grrr. Stop thinking about home.*

Alex nodded. "It's one of the company's strengths."

He went on to describe the benefits of living in northern California, but when lunch ended, Taylor felt she'd lost some of her enthusiastic glow while trying to fight the rising tide of love for Will.

◈

How could he miss her so much? He'd lived the past ten years without her; now her sudden presence in his life drilled into the very core of his being, and he felt lost without her.

The matters of the heart confounded him. Anxiety threatened.

What if she took the California job?

Will took a deep breath. "Be anxious for nothing," he prayed; "let the peace of Jesus guard your heart and mind."

Feeling restless, he wandered from his living room to the kitchen to the back porch. Harry sat watching, his head tipped in wonder.

"We need Taylor, don't we, boy?"

Harry whined, wagging his tail. When the phone rang, Will answered on the second ring with a deep hope that Taylor would be on the other end.

"I'm hungry for some of Sam's pie." It was Ethan.

"Pie?" Will echoed. "I could go for a big salad and soup."

"Eat whatever you want. I'm having pie."

Will laughed. "Don't worry, I'm having pie, too, but I haven't eaten dinner yet."

"It's eight o'clock."

"I know. Meet you there."

At Sam's, Will found his cousin in a booth by the door. Sam greeted him while Taylor's nephew set water glasses on the table.

"Have you heard from your aunt?" Will asked Jarred.

"Nope," the young man said with a quick, shy smile.

After they ordered, Ethan asked, "Speaking of Taylor, how's it going?"

Will shrugged as he unwrapped his silverware from the napkin. "It's not."

"She's still determined to move to California?"

"Yes, and still determined not to fall in love with me."

Ethan laughed. "And how do you know that?"

"She told me."

seventeen

From the balcony of her hotel, Taylor looked out over Coastal Highway 1, awed by the blazing colors of the Pacific sunset.

"Oh, Lord," she whispered reverently, "what a beautiful day." During her end-of-day wrap-up with Alex, he asked Taylor about her earliest possible start date while informing her of their generous relocation package.

"What's your minimum salary?" he asked, a smug sort of look on his face.

Taylor exhaled. She took his pen and jotted down a fat figure—ten percent more than she'd earned in New York.

Alex didn't even flinch. "Not a problem."

Now, on the balcony at her hotel with a cool breeze carrying the scent of the ocean brushing her face, Taylor pondered her options.

"Lord, do I say yes if they offer?" She loved what she heard and saw at Boswell Global. She loved the idea of living in sunshine and making a six-figure salary. Before she turned thirty-four, she would have accomplished more than she'd hoped.

She was envisioning Saturdays on the beach just as her room phone rang. "Hello?"

"Taylor, it's Alex Cranston."

She sank onto the bed. A nervous knot tightened in her middle. "I didn't expect to hear from you so soon."

Were they turning her down already?

"I just called to see how you like your room."

"It's very nice." She chewed on her bottom lip.

"Well, you're our front-runner. They loved you."

"That's good to hear." She sat against the hotel bed's plump pillows.

"As far as the president is concerned, you're the one. I had to remind her we'd already scheduled interviews with the other candidates."

Taylor smiled. "Pamela and I had a lot of common experiences and thoughts on how the finances should be run."

"That's what she said. She can't imagine anyone fitting the bill as well as you do. But we still—"

"I know. Interview the other candidates."

"Right. Have a good night. Order room service, watch a movie, and have a safe trip home. We'll send a car for you in the morning to take you to the airport."

"Thank you, Alex, for all you've done for me." When Taylor hung up, she thought she should jump for joy over Pamela's favor. Instead, she wandered back to the balcony feeling melancholy.

In the last few months, she'd gotten used to the safe comfort of being home. In the early morning, she would lie in bed praying and listening to her parents' morning routine.

"Grant, do you want coffee?"

Her mother's intonations were like Taylor's down comforter— soft and warm.

"Yes, Trixie. No cream this morning."

Her father always answered from the top of the stairs while dressing for the day. Taylor knew because the clean scent of his aftershave perfumed the hall and seeped into her room under the door.

California—three thousand miles away and a six-hour plane ride.

She leaned on the balcony rail, longing to talk to someone. She thought of her friends in New York. Strange, how she'd lost touch with them so quickly. Except Reneé. Taylor sighed. This wasn't about Reneé or her friends in the city. It was about calling Will.

Whether she liked it or not, he'd taken up residence in her heart as her closest friend. She couldn't deny it any longer. He simply was her best friend.

With a decisive step across the room, she dug her cell phone from her purse and dialed. She shivered when he answered the phone.

"Hi, it's Taylor."

≈

Will was cutting the end of his apple pie a la mode when his cell phone jingled. "Will Adams."

He did not expect to hear her voice on the other end. He dropped his fork and cut a glance at Ethan.

"So, you got the job?" he asked, running his hand through his hair.

"They liked me a lot."

"I believe it." He ignored the stab of disappointment. He was happy for her but sad for himself. "How's California?"

"Beautiful. The sunset is amazing. You'd love it here."

"I bet I would." Because she was there.

Taylor talked about her day with enthusiasm—the wonderful staff at Boswell Global, the funny story the president told during their interview, lunch at the cutest pizza place, and her hotel balcony overlooking the Coastal Highway.

"Sounds wonderful."

"I don't think I can say no." Taylor blurted the amount of her possible salary.

Will whistled.

"What? What's she saying?" Ethan whispered, poking Will's arm with his fork.

Will jerked away and swerved in the booth so Ethan couldn't hear. He felt vulnerable, as if his emotions might explode and spew all over the place.

"Hard to turn that down."

"R—right."

The conversation lulled. Will choked back a mountain of words, but how could he say again what he'd already said? Taylor had turned him down cold. "When will you know?"

"Week or so, I guess."

Will managed one word. "Good."

"They have more candidates to interview, but the president really wants to hire me."

"He knows excellence when he sees it."

Taylor laughed. "She. The president is a she. Pamela Carlton."

"Ah, forgive me." He faced forward again and reached for his fork.

"Oh, Will, I can see some kids playing on a basketball court." Excitement buoyed her voice.

He cut a bite of pie. "Who's winning?"

"Hard to tell. There's a couple of kids playing. One is dribbling. Stops to shoot a three-pointer. He makes it." Taylor cheered the unknown player, her voice vibrant.

"Well, maybe if I visit you in California, we can play one-on-one on that court."

She didn't answer for a moment, then said, "I'd like that."

"We'll miss you." He had to say it. He wanted her to know. So, he masked his *I* with a *we*, but she knew.

"We? You and Harry."

He grinned. "Yes."

"Well, I'll let you go. Thanks for listening."

"Is that all?"

"I guess so."

Will pressed END and placed the phone into the holster clipped to his belt. "That was Taylor," he said.

Ethan eyed him. "I gathered."

Will shoved his plate aside, missing Taylor more each minute.

≈

Thanksgiving Eve, Taylor tossed and turned, trying to sleep, her mind troubled by a myriad of anxious thoughts.

She prayed intermittently, meditating on the peace of Jesus. Her interview in California seemed like years ago.

Since she'd returned to White Birch and Lambert's Furniture, she'd been working fourteen hours a day. The data conversion to the HBS system aggravated her, and today had been especially trying.

In the morning, she'd battled technical problems with the test database. In the afternoon, she and Markie ran a test conversion, and all the fields were populated with the wrong information. Then, just before leaving for the night, she and Markie ran into a snag with the accounts receivable modules, and she feared they didn't work the way HBS promised.

Taylor sat up in bed and glanced at the clock. Nearly midnight. She reached for her bedside lamp.

The crash course she'd gotten from the installation team generated more questions than answers. And when they flew through the instructions on how to connect to the test and live databases, Taylor's notes began to look like ancient Chinese.

If I wasn't connected to the right database, then the system settings would be wrong. She sat with her arms on her knees. She felt lost on this one and feared she was letting Will down.

She slipped out of bed and changed into a pair of jeans and a university sweatshirt. She had to fix the problem. She tied on her running shoes.

The office was closed Thursday and Friday for the holiday, so she'd have the place to herself all weekend if she wanted to work.

Maybe Will didn't count on her long-term, but she wanted to complete the job with excellence. She'd dealt with new installations before, and the amount of overlooked details could be staggering.

Tiptoeing downstairs, Taylor picked up her purse and grabbed her coat.

Under a blanket of night, White Birch slept.

Maintenance crews had hung Christmas decorations yesterday afternoon and the front windows of Main Street shops twinkled with tiny white lights.

Suspending her thoughts for a moment, Taylor imagined she lived in a land far, far away where love conquered all and hearts were never broken.

She decided she must be longing for heaven. The idea touched her soul with peace as she passed White Birch

Community Church and steered toward Lambert's Furniture.

She parked by the side office door, punched in her security code on the keypad, and dashed upstairs to her office.

Within fifteen minutes, she'd found the problem with her settings and had successfully run a partial test of the data conversion.

She clapped her hands and did a little jig around her desk. Still wide-awake, she thought she might as well work on modifying reports before going home.

Footfalls echoed from the hallway. Taylor rose slowly from her chair, angling to see beyond her door, a cold feeling washing over her.

ֶֶ

Will couldn't sleep. He checked his bedside clock for the tenth time in the last half hour. After midnight. With a sigh, he stepped out of bed and wandered past the sleeping dog to the window.

In the moon's pale light, he surveyed his yard, half in the moon's glow, half falling into shadow.

"It's Thanksgiving and I'm fretting." He clicked on a light and reached for his Bible.

The words from Philippians 4:6 reminded him that the Lord watched over him.

He repeated the verse out loud. "Be anxious for nothing, but in everything by prayer and supplication, with thanksgiving, let your requests be made known to God."

Will paced the width of his bedroom. His day had been so fragmented by meetings, phone calls, interviews for a new administrator in accounting, plus a production meeting with Grandpa and Grant, that he felt burdened by the unattended details on his desk.

He stopped pacing and muttered to no one, "Might as well get dressed and go to the office."

As he pulled up to Lambert's Furniture, he expected to see a dark building, but the corner office glowed with a low, white light. Will smiled. Taylor.

"Wonder what she's doing here." He punched in his security code and bounded up the stairs.

❧

Taylor's heart beat so fast she had to draw hard to breathe. She looked around for something to use as a weapon.

"Settle down, Taylor Jo, the building is secure." She checked her watch. Who could be there at twelve thirty in the morning?

The steps drew closer. She blurted, "Hello?"

Will's handsome form came through her doorway. "What are you doing here?"

Taylor slapped her hand over her heart. "Oh, it's you."

Will grinned. "I've got to stop scaring you."

"Yes, you do." Taylor sat down in her desk chair. "What are *you* doing here?"

Will crossed his arms and leaned against the doorframe. "I asked you first."

The collar of his leather jacket was flipped up on one side, and his bangs flopped over his forehead. Taylor thought he looked like an eighties pop star—and very handsome.

He caught her staring. She blushed and turned away. "I, um, couldn't sleep. Problem with the conversion setup kept me awake. I finally figured it out."

Will walked over. "Funny how brilliance comes at midnight."

She laughed. "Yes." Their eyes met, and Taylor felt warm all the way down to her toes.

He stepped closer, his gaze never leaving her face. She couldn't breathe for a second.

"Taylor," he said, lightly grasping her arm and pulling her to him. He lowered his face to hers.

"Will." She pressed her hand against his chest.

He chuckled. "You drive me crazy, you know that?"

"I'm sorry."

Releasing her, he backed away. "Don't be. It's my problem. But, Taylor," he said as he walked toward the door, "when a man finds a woman who drives him crazy, he doesn't easily forget."

eighteen

Taylor bolted upright when her cell phone rang. She fumbled through her purse, squinting in the bright morning light. Sun rays streamed through the frosty windowpanes like ethereal ribbons and fell across the wide wood floor.

"Hello," Taylor croaked, rubbing the sleep from her eyes.

"Taylor, where are you?"

"Tim? I'm at the office," she said, her voice raspy and weak. She stood to stretch. Her back ached.

"Mom called this morning."

"What happened?"

"It's Dad. He woke up with severe abdominal pain, chills, and vomiting, so Mom took him to the hospital. She looked for you, but thought you went for a run."

"I'm on my way." Awake now, she grabbed her coat and purse but stopped outside her office door, suddenly overwhelmed. Her eyes burned, and she trembled all over.

"It's Thanksgiving. Oh, Father, please. Be with Dad."

Shaking off the sense of despair, she started down the hall.

⁂

Will looked up when he heard footsteps. *Is Taylor still here?* He glanced at his watch. Seven a.m. He'd fallen asleep a few times, brewed and drank two pots of coffee, then continued working. A lot of things were going to change with the new business system and work flow, even timekeeping and payroll.

"Taylor?"

She peered around the door bleary-eyed, her hair in disarray. "Mom took Dad to the hospital." Taylor explained his symptoms.

Will grabbed his coat. "Let's go." He unclipped his cell

phone and dialed as he led Taylor downstairs and out the door.

"Bobby, I'm on my way to the hospital with Taylor. It's Grant. Call Grandpa and let the family know. And, oh, will you go let Harry out, then take him to Grandpa's?"

He opened the passenger door and helped Taylor in. Then, getting in behind the wheel, he said, "It's going to be okay."

She nodded, her lips pressed together, the tip of her sleek nose red.

Will scooted across the seat and cradled her in his arms. He didn't know if she would resist and pull away, but he didn't care. She was trying too hard to endure this alone.

After a few moments, he reluctantly released her and moved back to his side of the truck. "Not a great way to start Thanksgiving Day, is it?"

"No, it isn't."

❦

By midmorning, Dad had been admitted and several tests ordered.

Taylor paced the waiting room with Tim and Mom. Dr. Griswold promised an update within the hour. Will went to the cafeteria in search of coffee and donuts.

"I can't lose him. I'm not ready. He's only sixty-six," Mom said, her voice weak like a lost child's.

Tim stood off on his own, his hands on his hips. "He'll be fine, Mom."

Taylor glared at him. He sounded like a coach telling a player to get up and shake it off.

"Mom," she said softly, putting her hand on her shoulder. "Tim's right. Dad is going to be just fine. We just have to trust in the Lord."

Mom pressed her hand on Taylor's. "Be brave for me, okay?"

Taylor rested her cheek on her mother's head. "I'll try."

Will returned with the coffee and donuts, followed by Bobby, Ethan, and their grandparents, Matt and Betty.

"Looks like the Lord sent in the cavalry," Will said, motioning to his family.

"Yes, He has," Mom said, welcoming Grandma Betty's embrace.

"Thank you," Taylor whispered to him as he handed her a cup of coffee and a donut. "Your family is amazing."

She didn't resist when he slipped his arm around her and kissed her tenderly on the forehead.

Grandma Betty took over comforting Mom, reminding Trixie Hanson that the Lord would not forsake her. Taylor loved the older woman's wise, soothing ways.

Grandpa motioned for everyone to huddle up. "Let's take this matter to the Father."

Will took Taylor's hand when Grandpa started to pray. "Lord, Your Word says You give us peace. Not as the world does, but the kind that transcends understanding. You said we must not let our hearts be troubled or fearful. So I ask for Your peace to guard Trixie and the Hanson family. Especially Grant."

Dr. Griswold approached as Grandpa said amen. "Well, Trixie, we know what's going on."

She wiped her eyes with the edge of her handkerchief. "Oh?"

Taylor felt a release in her middle, as if she'd been carrying a weight around all morning. Her hand remained in Will's, but she didn't care.

"Looks like food poisoning," the doctor said. "We're going to treat him overnight, but he's going to be fine. Do you know where he ate last night?"

"We had seafood," Trixie said, giving Dr. Griswold the name of the restaurant.

The doctor smiled. "Well, we'll make sure he's feeling better soon, but keep those prayers coming."

"Thank you, Doctor, we will," Grandpa said, his arm around Trixie's shoulders. Doctor Griswold offered to take Trixie to see Grant while the rest of the Hansons figured out how to celebrate Thanksgiving.

"Dad would want us to celebrate," Tim decided.

"We have a big spread at our house," Grandma said. "The girls are basting the turkey as we speak."

So it was agreed. The Hansons would join the Lamberts for a Thanksgiving feast.

⋙

Luscious smells wafted from Grandma's kitchen as Will tussled on the living room floor with Bobby's boys, Jack and Max. From Grandpa's easy chair, Will's dad, Buddy, coached the boys.

"Get your arm around Will's neck, Jack. Yeah, that's it."

When the six-year-old almost pinned his uncle, Will raised his head and asked his dad, "Whose side are you on, anyway?"

"My grandson's, of course."

"All right, all right." Will grabbed Jack by the ankles and dangled him upside down. "Say 'Uncle Will's the best.' "

Jack giggled. "No."

Will shook him. "Say it?"

Still giggling, Jack refused.

"Well, I have no alternative but to tickle you." A slight move of Will's hand and Jack caved.

"Uncle Will's the best. Uncle Will's the best."

Will lowered him to the floor. "Go bug your dad and Ethan."

Laughing, Jack scurried off to the family room where Bobby, Ethan, and Kavan watched football.

Four-year-old Max trailed after him, calling out, "Uncle Will's the best!"

Will sat on the floor and propped himself against the sofa. "That wore me out."

His dad chuckled. "I remember when you and Bobby used to jump on me. Two of you. Same size. Same weight."

Will took a deep breath, grinning. "My apologies, Dad."

Buddy shook his head. "Wouldn't trade those days for all the gold in Fort Knox."

Grandpa peered around the corner. "Buddy, you up for carving a turkey?" Grandpa held up his carving knife.

Buddy slapped his hands on his knees. "If it gets us closer to dinner, I'm your man."

Will waved. "Call me when it's time to eat."

As Buddy went off with Grandpa, Claire and Taylor walked by with Jack's eight-year-old sister, Eva.

Will waved at Taylor, and she answered with a smile. Her presence messed with him. Loving her came easy, like she was a part of him. If he thought about it long enough, his desire turned into a steady ache.

But she set up invisible boundaries, and he had no choice but to respect them.

He winced every time he thought about the night she asked him to marry her. It changed their relationship forever. If he knew then what he knew now, he wondered if he would have agreed.

But he doubted it. He'd needed the years to mature and discover who he was in this life and in Christ.

He would have made a lousy husband at twenty-three. Suddenly, Taylor dropped down next to him.

"Having fun?"

"Yes, are you?" He loved the cool fragrance that surrounded her.

She stared at her hands. "As long as I don't think too much about Dad."

He reached for her hand. "Grant is going to be fine."

"I know, I know." She looked over at him. "It's wonderful being here. So peaceful. Mom's busy in the kitchen with Grandma, your mom, Elizabeth, and Julie. Dana's playing with baby Matt—and I think trying to talk Tim into one last child."

Will laughed. "How's he taking it?"

Taylor shook her head and made a face. "Not well. Not well at all." She laughed.

"Taylor, I want you to know that—"

"Dinner! Let's go," Grandpa bellowed from the hall.

Taylor drew her hand from Will's and stood. "Let's eat."

He grabbed her and whispered, "You're determined to drive me crazy, aren't you?"

৯

"All right, who's up for a little flag football?" Ethan pushed back his chair and surveyed the table.

Bobby's boys shouted, "Me!" and scrambled from the table.

"Easy, boys," Elle called after them.

Taylor grinned. "They're good kids, Elle."

She nodded. "Thank you. They're trying at times, but I can't imagine life without them."

"Come on, who else?" Ethan cajoled the others. "You can't leave me with a four- and six-year-old."

Julie laughed. "Please, somebody play with him. He's been dreaming of this all week."

Bobby sighed and slapped his napkin on the table. "I'll regret this tomorrow, but I'm in."

Tim, Jarred, and Quentin agreed to play.

Will downed the last of his tea. "I'll get the football and organize the little guys." He looked at Taylor. "You playing?"

She glanced at the long table loaded with dirty dishes. "No, I'll help in here."

Grandma held up her hands. "Now, Taylor, I've got a room full of women who couldn't care less about playing flag football. You go ahead. We can handle this."

Elizabeth and Julie egged her on. "Yeah, Taylor, give those boys a run for their money."

"Well." She stood, unable to hide her grin. "I guess I can play."

Eight-year-old Eva piped up. "I want to play." Her big, blue-eyed gaze shifted to Claire. "Are you playing?"

Claire cut a glance at Taylor. "Should I?"

Laughing, Taylor slipped her arm around her niece and smoothed her hand over Eva's dark hair. "Absolutely."

"This game needs a referee," Buddy said. "Besides, I need to work off some of this turkey so I have room for pie."

"Everyone who's playing, go on," Grandma commanded. "We'll clean up and have pie later."

❧

"Down! Set! Hut, hut, hut!"

Jarred snapped the ball to Will. He dropped back to pass, his sights on his brother.

But the opposition rushed hard, mainly Taylor, and he had to scramble to keep from losing the blue flags tucked into his waist.

"You're mine, Adams," she shouted, running after him.

On the run, he cut to the right. "Don't tease me, Hanson. Bobby, get open!"

Ethan ran circles around Bobby, waving his arms in his face.

"Bob, come on! Shake him!" Will shouted, laughing. Just as he drew his arm back to pass, he stumbled, with Taylor on his heels and lunging for his flag.

Thud!

"Ouch!"

Will looked behind him as he released the ball.

"Taylor, what happened?" He looked down at the svelte, athletic brunette lying on the ground, her hand over one eye.

"You elbowed me."

He pinched his lips together to keep from guffawing and knelt on one knee. "Let me see." He pulled her hand away. A dark, reddish ring circled her eye.

"Oh, baby, I'm so sorry."

"No, it's not your fault. All's fair in war and football. Is it a shiner?"

He smiled, cupping her chin in his hand. "A beaut." Gently, he touched the bruised area. "Does that hurt?"

She swallowed. "No." Her fingers gripped his hand.

"Liar." Will tipped his head and gently kissed her eye. Then her cheek. Then her lips.

nineteen

Sunday morning Taylor dressed for church, her mind made up. No more Will Adams kisses. No more romantic interludes. No more football. No more walks down memory lane. The past is in the past and should be left there. They couldn't recapture ten-year-old emotions. It was ridiculous to try. Life moved on, and so should they.

Her face felt hot when she thought of his Thanksgiving Day kiss in the Lamberts' backyard. Everyone saw them.

"A weak moment," she muttered, brushing mascara on her lashes. "I let the man who gave me a black eye kiss me."

In spite of herself, she laughed. "It *was* funny." She leaned in to get a closer look at her eye. The swelling had gone down and now, with makeup, she could barely see the dark circle.

"Taylor, I'm going on ahead. I have to set up for Sunday school refreshments," Mom called up the stairs.

Taylor stuck her head out the door. "Okay."

Mom said to Dad, "We'll be home right after church, Grant."

Grant answered, "The weatherman said it's going to snow, so don't dally after services."

Taylor smiled. She would miss these exchanges when she moved to California. "Come on, Alex Cranston, call with the offer."

ঽ

Peace and warmth filled the church sanctuary. Taylor took an aisle seat as the pastor opened the service with a prayer.

"Scoot over."

She looked up at Will's handsome face. With a grimace, she made room.

"How are you?" he whispered, turning her face to his with a touch on her chin. "Your eye looks good."

"I'm fine." She pulled away from him. His two-second presence melted all her resolve to move on without him.

One whisper, one touch, and she found herself remembering his kiss and longing for another.

She squeezed her eyes shut and bowed her head. *Lord, take this away.*

Up front, Jeremiah strummed his guitar, opening the worship service by exalting the name of Jesus. Will's smooth baritone washed over her.

Oh, Will! There were too many wonderful things about him. Why couldn't he have said yes ten years ago?

Taylor tried to focus, tried to worship the One who loved her and deserved all her adoration. But Will's presence almost overwhelmed her.

She had to get out of there. Picking up her purse, she pressed her hand on Will's arm. "Excuse me."

Surprised, he asked, "Where are you going?"

"California."

❧

By late afternoon, snow had covered the town in a blanket of white.

Will lit the gas logs in his fireplace and settled in his recliner to read, but he couldn't focus. He read a whole chapter without comprehending one word.

With a sigh, he closed the book, walked over to the window, and watched the snow gently falling.

Harry nudged Will's leg. "This is your kind of weather, isn't it?"

The dog barked once, loudly.

Will laughed. "Guess we could go out for a walk."

Harry yipped at the word "walk" and wagged his tail. Once outside, the huge sheepdog romped in the snow like a puppy. Snow fell steadily, and with every step, Will plowed a new path.

After an hour, he beckoned Harry with a whistle. "Come on, boy, let's go home."

As he turned toward home, the path he'd plowed to this

point was already covered in snow.

A reflection of my life with Taylor, he mused. Just when he thought he'd made headway with her, he found he'd left no imprint on her heart at all.

"Lord, am I like that with You? So calloused at times that Your touch on my life is buried and hidden?"

Will stood in the moment, praying, yearning to yield more of his heart to the Lord's touch. Taylor or no Taylor, he was nothing without the love of Jesus.

In the quiet, with Harry panting softly next to him, the familiar peace of Jesus fell on him. He understood the Lord commanded his life—even his relationship with Taylor.

"You can have all of me. Even my love for Taylor." The words stung for a moment, but Will determined to make Jesus Lord over every area of his life.

From the twilight horizon, Will heard the music of sleigh bells. He turned to greet Jamis Willaby.

"Nice day for a sleigh ride, don't you think?" Jamis called out. "Whoa, boy."

Will slipped off his gloves and touched the horse's velvety nose. "Is this Polo?"

"Yep," Jamis said with a nod, his breath billowing about his head. "Son of Marco."

The horse tossed his head with a snort as if he understood, the bells ringing.

Will laughed. "Beautiful sleigh." He walked back toward Jamis. "The craftsmanship is excellent."

"My granddaddy made it. Don't get to use it much, but I couldn't resist today. The salt trucks will be out soon and by tomorrow the sleigh won't be able to go the roads."

"You're right. Nothing like a romantic—" Will stopped abruptly. "Say, Jamis, how much to rent the sleigh?"

The older man laughed. "Nothing. You need to borrow it?"

"Just for tonight."

Jamis moved over and motioned for Will to hop in. "I'll give you the two-second lesson."

Taylor stood back, her hands on her hips. "A little more to the right, Tim."

He pushed on the tree.

"No, now that's too much," Mom said. "Back to the left."

Tim peered at them through the blue spruce tree's branches. "Would you two make up your minds?"

Taylor spread her arms. "We are. You're moving it too much. Just a half inch to *your* left."

The spruce moved slightly.

"Perfect," the ladies said in unison.

"Okay, Taylor, hold it in place while I tighten the bolts," Tim said.

Taylor hurried over. "This is fun. I haven't decorated a Christmas tree in ages."

"Really, Taylor, you should slow down and enjoy life a little," Mom said.

"One day, Mom, one day."

"Hot chocolate." Dana carried a tray from the kitchen. "Jarred, Quentin, Claire, hot chocolate."

The boys shut down the video game, but Claire remained at the kitchen counter, cell phone pressed to her ear.

"How about some Christmas music?" Taylor suggested.

"Got it, Aunt Taylor." Quentin moved to the stereo.

Taylor picked up two mugs and handed one to her father as she sat next to him on the family room sofa.

"You think Boswell Global is going to make you an offer?" Tim asked, perched on the edge of the love seat with a steaming mug in his hand. "Claire, hang up and join the family."

"She's in love," Dana said, sitting down next to her husband.

"With whom?" Taylor asked, her eyes wide.

"Zach Maybrey. Nice boy—very cute."

"Is that the boy she asked me about several weeks ago?"

"Probably," Dana said.

Tim called to his daughter again. "Claire, come on, off the phone."

"Shh, Tim, she's eighteen."

Tim sat back. "Don't remind me."

Dad laughed. "Never had to worry much about Taylor and boys. Only one she ever hung around with was Will, and I'd trust him any day."

Tim laughed. "Yeah, did you hear about the Thanksgiving Day kiss?"

Taylor jumped in. "All right, change the subject. Yes, Tim, I do think Boswell will offer me the job."

Mom entered from down the hall, her arms loaded with ornaments. She set them on the coffee table with a sigh. "Jarred, please do your old grandma a favor and bring the rest out."

"Help him, Quent," Dana said.

The boys scurried away. Claire walked past her dad, kissing him on the cheek. "I'm off the phone. You happy?" She plopped down next to Taylor.

"Yes," Tim said.

"So, are we talking about Will and Taylor's kiss?"

Taylor leapt to her feet. "No, we are not. Time to decorate the tree. Claire, help me with the lights."

"Taylor," Dad said, moving slowly off the couch. "Can I talk to you?" He motioned to the living room.

"See what you've done now?" she said over her shoulder to Tim then whispered to Claire, "If he grounds me, I'm running away from home."

Claire laughed.

In the living room, Dad clicked on a low light. "What's this kiss business? I thought you two were just friends."

She blushed. "He kissed me." Taylor fell to the couch and hugged a throw pillow, flipping the fringe between her fingers.

"He loves you."

She hopped up. "That's his problem." Her tone was deep and solid. "I've made my position clear. I'm not grabbing some romantic thread left dangling in the corridor of time. If I pull on it, my whole life unravels."

"Or, your whole life is finally sewn up, neatly pieced together."

"Har, har. Very funny." Taylor tried to frown, but a smile tugged at her lips. "I'm pressing forward to what lies ahead, Dad. I'm thirty-three, at the crux of my career. If I don't get going soon, I'll be left behind. Technology changes so fast, companies reorganize on a whim. Dot-coms die overnight. Boswell Global is on the rise, and I want a California job with a big fat salary."

Dad tipped his head in understanding. "You're at the crux of love, too, Taylor. True love and men like Will are hard to find. I know you're determined to get this California job, but I'm warning you, as your father and friend, make sure. Look deep."

Tears burned in her eyes. "I'm sure, Dad. I'm sure."

He regarded her. "For some reason, I don't think you are."

"Taylor!" Claire ran into the room. "You have to come see this."

"See what?" Taylor followed her back into the family room and looked out the open side door.

There, standing in an old sleigh, was Will.

"Would you like to go for a ride?"

She pressed her hand over her mouth, hiding a big grin. He looked amazingly cute with his dark bangs flopping over a skier's headband.

The sleigh bells rang out as the horse shook his head. Harry answered with a sharp bark.

Will grinned. "I brought Harry along to chaperone."

Say no. No, Taylor. No. "Well, the family is here. We're decorating the tree—ouch," she said, rubbing the spot where Claire's sharp fingernail had jabbed her in the side.

"She'll be right out, Will."

Claire pulled her away from the door. "Get your coat. You may be moving to California, but you never pass up a romantic sleigh ride with a man as incredibly wonderful and good-looking as Will Adams."

"Claire, please. You're a young fool in love." Taylor stomped up the steps, Claire's hand pressing against her back.

"Say what you will, but if I were seven or eight years older, I'd be making goo-goo eyes at Will myself."

"Whatever. And I never make goo-goo eyes." Taylor yanked her coat from the hanger.

"Well, maybe you should."

Taylor zipped up her coat and sighed. "How do I look?"

"Beautiful. Now get going."

"Okay, okay. But, Claire, I'm not falling in love with Will. Been there, done that—not doing it again. In fact, this is the last time I'm hanging out with him."

"Yeah, you're like Dad. You say a lot of things."

❧

"It is beautiful," Taylor said, settling next to him with a deep sigh.

"You sound content." Will switched the reins from his right hand to his left, and despite the pump of adrenaline, he gingerly slipped his arm around her shoulders. She squared her shoulders, bumping his hand away, but he dropped it back into place, and after a few moments, she relaxed and leaned against him. Sort of.

"What a great way to start the Christmas season," she said. "Decorating the tree with the family and a sleigh ride with a friend."

"Sorry to interrupt your tree decorating."

Taylor nestled closer to him. "Are you kidding? The family practically kicked me out the door when you showed up."

He grinned. "So I noticed."

Taylor rested her head against his shoulder, and he wondered if she could hear his heartbeat beneath his coat.

"They think I'm in love with you."

"Are you?"

"No," she said with a *hmm* in her voice. "But you smell nice."

twenty

Polo held his head high as he followed a moonlit path down Main Street. Will held the reins loosely in his left hand, guiding Polo out of town, but wrapped his right arm tighter around Taylor.

"It's cold," she said, snuggling closer. For once, she didn't stop to check the wall surrounding her heart, guarding against the charms of Will Adams. It felt good to be near him, locked in his embrace. Just for tonight.

"Do you want to go home?" He pulled her closer.

She shook her head. "No. I'm having fun."

"Be careful; you might fall in love with me."

She peered up into his face. "I'll let you have your dream."

He laughed. "My dream? Oh, no, Taylor. My destiny. You are my destiny."

"That sounds like a line from a movie."

"It's from my heart." He brushed her cheek with his gloved hand, the leather reins dangling. "You *are* so beautiful."

Taylor's heart beat like thundering horses. "Please, Will." She closed her eyes and buried her face in his shoulder. Dreamy, romantic notions threatened her resolve. "I can't—"

"Or you won't?"

"Please," she muttered.

"I won't stop telling you how I feel."

She sat up. "Neither will I."

"Then I guess we're at a stalemate."

She looked down. "We want different things."

"I used to think about you living up in New York. I wondered what you were doing and how you were doing," he said.

"I wondered about you, too."

"But I didn't call."

140

Taylor shook her head. "Neither did I."

"We chose career over love, I guess," he said.

"So you have to understand why this job in California is so important."

"So you have to understand why having you here is so important to me."

She shoved him slightly. "Don't make fun of me."

He pulled her close. "Never. I'm using your words to get you to understand."

Suddenly Polo stopped. Taylor glanced up. "Where are we?"

Will laughed as he wrapped both arms around her. "The covered bridge."

***

They left Polo standing on the shoulder of the road and walked onto the bridge. "When do you think you'll hear from Boswell Global?" Will asked. He had to leave the subject of *them* before Taylor's stubborn streak made her refuse to even spend time with him.

Her breath billowed in the cold as she said, "This week, I think. It's been two weeks already."

He leaned against the railing. "You've been a big help to Lambert's Furniture."

"Markie is catching on very quickly. She's going to be key to the new system's success."

The cold prevented them from staying too long on the bridge. As they walked back to the sleigh, they talked about their favorite Christmases. "I think this is my favorite Christmas," Taylor admitted, as Will gathered the reins and chirruped to Polo. "I'm actually baking cookies with Mom tomorrow night."

Will smiled. "I think this is my favorite, too."

They rode in a comfortable silence with only the sound of Polo's bells jingling and jangling, until Taylor asked out of the blue, "Do you think a Yankee like me can survive in California?"

His laugh rang out. "You can survive anywhere. The Californians won't know what hit them."

Taylor punched him lightly, giggling. "Stop."

"I'm serious. When you're around, Taylor, the atmosphere changes."

She settled against him. "It must be Jesus in me, 'cause I'm not that special."

"You are very special, but you let Him shine. A lot of people don't."

"You do."

He snuggled closer to her. "I try."

"I wanted to tell you, you're a very good boss."

He smirked. "You're excellent at what you do, too. We'd make a great team, Taylor."

To Will's delight and surprise, she leaned into him and purposefully, softly kissed him while Polo drew the sleigh over mounds of fresh snow toward the moonlit horizon.

❧

Early Monday morning, Taylor sat under twinkling Christmas lights at Peri's Perk, picking at a cinnamon muffin, clicking her fingernails against the sides of her latte cup and reliving her kiss with Will for the hundredth time.

Not his kiss. *Her* kiss. She caved, weakened by a romantic setting, and kissed him. She felt like a walking contradiction, and her actions weren't fair to Will.

"Hello, Taylor."

She shifted to see Julie Lambert walking toward her, smiling.

"Julie, good morning." Taylor rose and gave the pretty blond a hug.

"Mind if I join you? I have a few minutes to sit before school starts."

Taylor smiled. "Please do."

She watched as Julie picked out a Danish and ordered coffee from Peri. Despite her feelings about her relationship with Will, Taylor loved the Lambert family.

She'd spent many summer nights eating Grandma Betty's barbecue, roasting marshmallows over an open pit, watching movies with the cousins, and playing basketball, football, and baseball.

"So, what is up with Taylor Hanson these days? By the way, you look fabulous." Julie settled on the high, round stool with her breakfast.

Taylor smiled. "Thank you, but I exercise too little and eat too much. Work too much."

Julie smiled. "Exercise? I see you running around town all the time. I have a treadmill that moonlights as a clothes hanger."

Taylor laughed. "It gets harder the older I get."

"Tell me about it," she said. "Between teaching at the elementary school, conducting private music lessons, and playing in a quartet, I never seem to find time to exercise."

"I'm surprised you and Ethan don't have a houseful of kids," Taylor said. "I hear they keep you running."

Julie's expression darkened, and she broke off the edge of her Danish without taking a bite. "Ethan and I can't have children."

"Oh, Julie, I'm sorry." Taylor's cheeks flushed.

With a small smile, Julie said, "No, it's okay. We are going to adopt next year."

Taylor rested her hand over her heart. "Wow, that's wonderful."

Julie leaned forward, placing her elbows on the table. "It was hard at first. . .when we found out. But life comes with unexpected curves and dead ends. The Lord has blessed us in so many other ways."

"Life does come with ups and downs, doesn't it?"

Julie paused for a moment, then said, "Ethan tells me you have a job opportunity in California."

Taylor sipped her coffee then bobbed her head yes.

"What about Will?" Julie asked, her expression pure and earnest.

"What about him?" Taylor retorted, gently setting her cup down.

"Honestly, Taylor. I mean, well, he's in love with you."

Taylor crossed her legs then uncrossed them. "What makes you say that?"

Julie laughed. "It's written all over his face. It was the talk of the kitchen cleanup crew Thanksgiving Day."

"We're keeping our relationship as friends."

Julie cocked one eyebrow. "Really? You know it's written all over your face, too."

Indignant, Taylor scoffed, "What's written on my face?"

"That you, my friend, are in love with Will Adams."

৵

Will headed to Ethan's office with a cursory glance down the hall toward Taylor's office. Her light was on, but he had yet to see her.

He'd been unable to sleep, so he'd taken an early run along the freshly salted White Birch streets, praying and asking for the Lord to intervene in his relationship with Taylor.

The memory of her kiss made his lips buzz, and he worried things would be uncomfortable when they saw each other.

When he knocked on Ethan's door, his cousin motioned for Will to come in.

"What's up?" Ethan reclined in his desk chair and locked his hands behind his head.

"Are those production reports right? We're up ten percent?"

Ethan nodded then said, "I just got off the phone with Julie."

Will crossed his arms and cocked his head to one side. "And she confirms our increased production?"

"She ran into Taylor at Peri's."

His heart thumped once. "That's nice."

"She asked Taylor about the two of you." Ethan's crooked, mischievous grin lit his face.

"Why would she do that?"

"Because the whole family can see that you two love each other."

Will rubbed his forehead with his fingers. "Can we forget about Taylor for a minute? About our production—"

"Can you forget about Taylor?" Ethan refused to let the topic fade.

"Can we get some *grown-up* work done?"

Ethan shook his head. "I'm telling you, Taylor—"

"Yes?" Taylor popped her head into Ethan's office. "Did you call me?" Her green eyes scanned the room.

Ethan laughed, slapping his knee.

"No," Will said, shooting a sharp glance at Ethan. "Sorry."

Taylor hesitated, looked Will in the eye for a lingering moment, then at Ethan. "What's so funny?"

"Nothing," Will said with a stifled smile when she looked back at him. Her gaze contained no emotion, as if her kiss never happened.

Taylor shrugged and continued down the hall.

Will leaned forward, placing his hands on Ethan's desk. "If you weren't my cousin, I'd fire you."

Ethan laughed. "Right…"

Will took a deep breath. "Can we get back to the business of Lambert's Furniture?"

twenty-one

A little before eight p.m., Taylor's cell phone rang. Bleary-eyed from staring at the computer screen for almost thirteen hours, she batted her eyes to clear the fog from her contact lenses and answered with a raspy hello.

A low laugh sounded in her ear. "Did I wake you?"

Taylor straightened. "No."

"Good. This is Alex Cranston."

"Yes, I recognize your voice." She got up to pace, resting her hand on the small of her back.

"Welcome to Boswell Global."

"Thank you." She checked her cheer to maintain a professional tone. "That's wonderful."

"Corporate wants you right away, Taylor."

"Before Christmas?" Taylor understood Boswell Global would own her once she signed on the dotted line.

"By December 11, actually. That'll give you the rest of this week and next to make arrangements and drive out."

"Of course." She didn't sound strong or confident. Not what Alex needed to hear.

Will's handsome face suddenly appeared in the doorway. He made an eating motion and whispered, "You want something to eat?"

Taylor held up one finger. To Alex she said, "Sounds good." For some reason, she didn't want Will to know. Not yet.

"I'll e-mail the formal offer. The salary is. . ."

Taylor gripped her middle when Alex said the amount—more than she'd asked for—and reminded her of their benefits package.

"Amazing," she said, tapping her fingers on the old polished desk. "Hard to turn down."

"They'll make you earn it."

"I can imagine."

A sharp memory of the corporate life stabbed at her. Long hours. Stress. Missed lunches. Fast-food dinners. Nonexistent personal life. She wondered if she was ready for the heavy commitment.

Will leaned against the door frame. He wore a navy button-down that matched his eyes. "Dinner?" he mouthed.

Taylor shrugged, listening to Alex, then shook her head no.

Will waited for a second, then left. For a brief, intense moment, she longed for him.

"So do I have a formal yes?" Alex prodded.

Taylor hesitated a fraction of a second. "Yes. You do. I accept."

"Excellent. Excellent. Listen, I've got a meeting, but why don't you give me a call tomorrow at your convenience, and we can talk start date and other details."

After saying good-bye to Alex, Taylor sat in front of the computer trying to remember what she was working on before his call.

But she couldn't. Unable to concentrate, she gave up, powered off her computer, and headed home, her emotions swirling with a mixture of exhilaration and anxiety.

⁂

Hands on his hips, Will looked at each face sitting at the boardroom table.

"What do you guys think?"

Bobby propped his elbows on the arms of his chair, his lips pursed. "I can't believe David Thomason called and offered us his business."

Ethan stood and walked around the long table. "This is amazing." He shook his head but smiled.

Grandpa agreed. "I've known David a long time. Thomason's produces quality furniture, but, Will, I'm sure his business practices are a mess."

Will nodded. "We'll perform a due diligence, of course.

Ethan, I'd like you to do one on his environmental practices. Are they up to code, etcetera."

Ethan reached for his palm computer. "Will do."

Grandpa rapped on the table with his knuckles. "Wait, Will, are you boys saying you want to buy Thomason's?"

Bobby pushed away from the table then picked up his papers and laptop. "I need to meet with a new distributor down in Boston." He glanced around the room. "I'm for it. Let's buy Thomason's if the price is right and the due diligence report is good."

"I agree," Ethan said.

Will grinned. "I'll call Dave and set up a meeting."

Grandpa stood. "I think you boys are making the right decision." He walked to the door. "I'm going to see how Grant's doing down in production."

"Thanks for coming in for this meeting, Grandpa." Will waved at him as the elder Lambert exited. Grant Hanson had returned to work a few days ago, rested and healed. He'd taken over his supervisory duties without missing a beat.

"You know, Will," Ethan started, returning to his chair, "we could really use Taylor to help us with the due diligence and merging these two companies."

Will ran his hand over his hair. "We could."

"I mean, we can manage, but she'd be invaluable."

"Except for one thing. She's moving to California."

"Why don't you just ask her to marry you and stop this silly dance?"

"She doesn't want to marry me, Ethan. I've told you that."

"Have you formally asked her to marry you?"

"No, but she's made it clear she's moving on."

"Will, put it out there. Ask her to marry you. All she can do is say no." Ethan reached for his palm computer and stood.

"Whose side are you on?"

Ethan laughed as he walked toward the door. "Yours."

Will walked down to Taylor's office, pensive. "Knock, knock," he said outside her door.

She smiled and waved him in, finishing her conversation with Markie. "I think we're going to have to require this field, or we could lose the order information."

Markie sighed. "I agree, but it's just more for us to fill out."

"I'll try to find a shortcut or create a quick key or something. But we're going to have to use it."

"Let me go play around with it, too." Markie stood. "Hi, Will," she said as she left.

Will sat next to Taylor in Markie's vacant seat. "How's it going?"

"Good. Making headway."

"David Thomason called. He offered to sell us Thomason's Furniture."

Taylor's eyes widened. "Will, that's incredible. Are you going to take him up on it?"

"Probably." He hesitated. "I'm here to offer you the job as CFO."

"You're kidding."

❧

Awake most of the night, fighting anxiety, Taylor mentally designed a new inventory work flow for the production department to use once the new business system went online.

She tried not to think of moving three thousand miles away—tried not to think of Will's job offer or the ever-present memory of the sleigh ride kiss.

Around three a.m., she tiptoed downstairs and microwaved a cup of hot chocolate. She prayed in the family room then sat quietly, staring at the red, blue, green, and white lights of the Christmas tree.

Jesus came to bring peace, but all she felt was anxious, tired, frayed, and jittery. At six a.m., she woke again after dozing on the couch. From the kitchen, she heard the sounds of Mom making breakfast. "Hey, sweetie," Dad said, peering into the family room. "Sleep on the couch?"

She got up, straightening and plumping the couch pillows. "I came down for hot chocolate and the Christmas lights."

She kissed him on the cheek as she passed, remembering how scared she was after his heart attack. What would life be without Grant Hanson? She didn't want to know.

From the stove, Mom offered to make Taylor a couple of eggs and toast.

"No thanks. I'm not hungry." Taylor went up to take a shower.

A little after lunchtime, in her Lambert's Furniture office, Taylor drew a deep breath and dialed Alex's number.

"Alex Cranston."

"Alex, hi, it's Taylor."

"Good morning."

She grinned. "Actually, it's afternoon here."

"Well, good afternoon then."

She rolled her eyes. He was far too chipper. "Yes, good afternoon."

He got right to business. "Here's the deal. We need you here by the eleventh." His words were firm, final.

"Is there any negotiation?" She bit her lower lip in anticipation.

"The January product launch is strategic to the company's financial goals, Taylor. I'm sure you understand the criticality of your involvement as CFO. You know—"

"Yes, I know." Taylor understood the meaning behind Alex's words. "I'll be there by the eleventh."

"Is there a critical reason why you need an alternate start date?"

"No." She sank to her chair. "Not really."

"Okay, good." His voice buoyed. "We'll put you up in a studio apartment until you find a place, and we'll take care of your initial food and other expenses."

"Of course." She forced a smile. "How's Christmas in California?"

"Beautiful."

"I'm sure it is." Maybe she could get her mom and dad to fly out so she wouldn't have to spend her first Christmas in California alone.

Wednesday night at church, the children's choir sang Christmas carols before the message. Little Susie Sharpton belted out "Away in a Manger" like a Broadway star.

Will applauded with the rest of the congregation, winking and waving at Jack and Max.

As Pastor Marlow blessed the children before they scurried away to children's church, Will felt a nudge on his arm.

"Move over."

He looked into Taylor's tired eyes. "You're working too hard," he whispered when she slid in next to him.

"Is that Max in the little suit?"

"Yes, and don't change the subject." He bumped her shoulder.

"I have a lot to do." Taylor bumped him back.

"Well, there's time. Don't kill yourself. Enjoy the holidays."

"Right."

Maybe it was his imagination, but Will thought he caught a flicker of sadness in her expression, just for a moment.

"There's a gathering at Grandma's after this."

"Thanks, but I think I'll go home."

He slipped his arm on the back of the pew and cradled her shoulders. "Cookies, eggnog, hot chocolate, warm fire, Christmas music, huge decorated tree. . ."

She shrugged away from his touch. "Shh, I'm listening to Pastor Marlow."

"Sorry." He pulled his arm back.

She propped her elbow on the pew's arm and rested her forehead in her hand.

Something had bothered her, Will could tell, for over a day now. He imagined it had something to do with the California job but didn't press her. He'd wait for her to open up in her way, in her time.

He whispered, "I'm here for you if you need me."

She nodded. "Thanks."

After the service, Will waited for Taylor outside the sanctuary doors. He felt awkward and a little like a desperate dog begging for a bone, but he'd decided to pursue Taylor until she married him. If she moved to California, he'd still pursue her, stopping only if she married someone else.

"It's cold tonight," he said, stepping in time with her.

He opened her car door for her after she pressed her remote access button.

Taylor peered into his eyes. "Thank you for being my friend."

"You're welcome." He leaned toward her, wanting to kiss her, but Trixie suddenly appeared.

"Taylor, darling, there you are."

Will smiled. Taylor's mother looked so perfect in her matching coat and shoes and a sixties-style pillbox hat on her head, no less. Only Trixie.

"We're all going to Betty and Matt's for cookies and hot chocolate."

Will cocked his right eyebrow with an I-told-you-so smirk.

Taylor made a funny face. "I'm tired, Mom."

"Well, of course; you've been working unseemly hours. I haven't seen you for three days. You must join us at the Lamberts'."

Grant hammered the last nail. "Come, Taylor. It's a family night."

She agreed with a muffled okay. When Trixie and Grant walked away, Will stepped around the car door and drew her into his arms.

Taylor burst into tears. He ached to help her, to understand what storm brewed beneath her smooth-as-glass exterior. But he didn't ask questions. He just let her cry as he cradled her head with his hand.

twenty-two

Every window of the Lamberts' home glowed with warm, golden light, and when Taylor turned into the driveway, she couldn't imagine being anywhere else right now.

Taking a moment to compose herself, she checked her face in the rearview mirror for mascara tracks and quieted her soul before the Lord.

"Father, You lead me. I'm not going to worry tonight."

Stepping out of the car, she saw Will walking her way, an oil lantern in his hand.

"What, out of flashlights?" She pointed to the lamp.

"No." He grabbed her hand. "It was on the porch. I grabbed the closest thing."

He led her to the house, his strong hand holding on to hers. If she could let her heart go for a moment, free to feel without consequence, Taylor would fall in love with him. She knew it.

He amazed her. His peace, his confidence, his unassuming manner. . .

Just beyond the front porch, he stopped. "It's a madhouse in there," he said, facing her.

She laughed. "I figured."

Two of the younger boys burst through the front door and thundered down the front steps, laughing and screaming.

"Oh, to be that carefree," Taylor said without preamble.

He chuckled. "Are you going to be okay?"

She nodded and dropped her head against his chest. "Sorry about earlier."

"Anytime. You've been working crazy hours."

"I want the installation to go well. Revenue is involved."

"Taylor, you've done a phenomenal job. Markie is begging me to find a way to keep you here."

She lifted her head to see his face. "I'm not sure you can afford me."

"I'm willing to try. The CFO job offer still stands." He brushed his cold hands along the sides of her face and hair.

"I know." She smiled and leaned into his touch.

"Can I kiss you?"

"Now you ask?"

He pulled her to him and gently pressed his lips to hers.

≈

The next morning, Taylor woke when her cell phone trilled. She looked at the clock on the nightstand. Nine o'clock!

She slapped her hand to her head. "I'm late." Scrambling out of bed, she reached for her phone. Probably Will.

"Is this Taylor Hanson?" a woman asked.

"Yes." Taylor hauled a pair of jeans and a sweater out of the dresser drawer.

"Wonderful," she said perkily. "This is Gretchen Levi from *Computing Today*."

Taylor jerked her head up. *"Computing Today"*?

"Yes, you're familiar with our magazine, right?"

Taylor swallowed. "Of course."

"Great. I'm doing a feature on women executives in dot-com companies. I'd love to feature the piece around you. Boswell Global's newest female exec and CFO."

They've sent out a press release already? "I haven't even started the job."

"Close enough in our book. This is a big coup for women in the dot-com world, Taylor. You're our icon." Gretchen's chipper voice grated on Taylor. Too early to be so cheerleader-like.

An hour later, Taylor hung up, finally finished talking with the gregarious Gretchen who'd asked a million questions. Thankfully, she didn't ask much about Blankenship & Burns.

While giggly, Gretchen proved to be a skilled reporter. Taylor felt a renewed excitement for her job.

≈

The story would run a week from Monday, hitting the streets

on her first day at Boswell. What a nice way to start her career there—in the news.

Walking toward her office, Taylor heard Will and Bobby laughing, Ethan's deep voice weaving through their merriment.

She stopped, thinking no place would feel like Lambert's Furniture. Family. Comfortable. Peaceful.

She decided to tell Will that Friday was her last day. She had to leave on Sunday. Was it that soon?

Markie had made great progress in the HBS installation, and right after Christmas, training started. Taylor felt she was leaving them in capable hands.

"Taylor, good morning." Will met her in the hall and placed his arm around her shoulder. "Sleep in?"

She laughed and flipped on her office light. "Yes. Guess I was tired."

"It's ten thirty." Will gave an over-exaggerated look at his watch. "Are you feeling okay?"

She set her purse on her desk and slipped out of her coat. "I need to talk to you."

"S—sure." He sat down.

A minute later, it was done. She told him. "Sunday, it's 'California, here I come.'"

He stared at her, his hands folded together in front of his face. "I can't believe you're going."

She couldn't look at him. Tracing her finger along the corner of her desk, she said, "It's an amazing opportunity. I never knew I could make so much money this soon in my career."

"I suppose it's especially sweet after New York." Will's words were strong, though his tone was low and soft.

Taylor nodded. "It is." Her gaze met his. "But thank you for the job here—and the CFO offer. I documented the procedures, setup, and work flows for the HBS system. They are stored out on the network." Taylor handed Will a single page of instructions.

He reached for it. "Thank you. I'll have Markie cut you a check." He started to say something but hesitated. "I'm not giving up on us." His voice was kind, but his words were sure.

Tears smarted in Taylor's eyes as Will walked out of her office. When her cell phone rang, she answered, grateful for the distraction. "Taylor Hanson."

"Congratulations! You got the job!"

She smiled, pressing on the edge of her eyes with her fingertips. "Indiana, hi. Yes, thanks to you."

"You're the industry buzz right now."

She set her hand on her waist. "What?"

"The word is you're the feature in *Computing Today's* next issue."

"Word travels fast."

"Lisa Downey, eat your heart out, eh?"

"No, Indiana, I wish her well," Taylor said. "She taught me a lot."

"Well, you're on to bigger and greener pastures," Indiana said.

"Right. Bigger, greener." Taylor glanced down the hall toward Will's office.

❧

"Are you sure?"

Will leaned toward Matilda, White Birch Bank's senior teller. "I'm sure."

She shook her head, muttering, "Well, I never," under her breath.

"First time for everything, Tildy," Will said with a wink.

"I've never known you to withdraw so much as a penny, let alone. . ."

Will tucked his money away, waved to the bank president, Fred Moon, and walked out the door.

Fresh snow drifted from low, gray clouds. Will tucked his coat collar around his neck and walked to his truck. Opening his door, he beckoned to Harry. "Come on, boy."

When he passed Duke's Barber Shop, he stuck his head in the doorway. "Need a haircut. I'll be back in about a half hour."

Duke waved from where he worked on Tom Laribee's balding head. "I'll hold my breath."

Will laughed and continued down Main Street, past Sam's. When he got to Earth-n-Treasures by Cindy Mae, he stopped and wiped his clammy hands down the sides of his khakis. He felt hot and nervous, yet peaceful and excited.

"Lord, here we go." Will was leaping out in faith, knowing the hand of the Lord would catch him. He had to take a chance; he had to risk it all.

"Will Adams." Cindy Mae looked up from her workbench on the far side of the shop. "I never thought I'd see you in here." She snorted.

He made a face. "You're seeing me now."

She hopped down from her large wooden stool, settling her hands on her wide, round waist. "What can I do for you? Something for your mom? Grandma Betty?" Harry nuzzled her leg, and she patted him on the head.

"No." Will pulled a printed Web page from his coat pocket. "I want this ring."

She whistled loud and long. "You're not going for cheap, are you?"

"I'd like to have it by Saturday."

"Saturday? What's this, an emergency engagement?"

He cleared his throat. "Can you have it by Saturday?"

"Let me do some checking. Be right back." She maneuvered her large frame toward the back office. "There are some dog treats over by the door if Harry wants one."

Will pulled a crunchy bone from a plastic container and gave it to his furry companion.

His blood pumped. He'd discovered the ring about a month ago while surfing the Web. If a man could fall in love with jewelry, he guessed he had with this ring. Elegant and modern, bold and beautiful, it was a platinum and diamond representation of Taylor Hanson.

This is crazy. But at the very core of his being, Will knew he had to ask Taylor to marry him. Ethan was right. He'd said everything but "Will you marry me?"

"I have two options for you," Cindy Mae said, coming

toward him. "I can get this ring in by tomorrow afternoon." She held up the picture Will gave her. "Or, I have this piece here." Cindy Mae held up a black, felt-covered ring box.

Will took it from her and pulled the ring from the slit. It was beautiful.

"Same karat weight as the one in the picture. Brill and I picked it up at an estate sale last summer. Belonged to ole Martin G. Snodgrass."

Will snapped his head up. "The old bachelor?"

Cindy Mae nodded. "One and the same. He fell in love with Carrie Waterhouse back in the sixties. But she was a wild child and ran off to California to make it in the movies."

Cindy Mae's words pelted him like hailstones. "Ran off to California." He put the ring in the box and thrust it at her.

"No thanks."

Cindy Mae gently closed the box's lid. "It's a beautiful ring, Will. Cheaper than the one you wanted."

"It's not the money," he said, looking her in the eye. He wanted something new. Something fresh. A ring that had never been slipped on a woman's finger with the words "Will you marry me?"

He didn't want a ring that signified a man's broken heart, a ring that signified a woman running off to California. He didn't want to be another Martin G. Snodgrass.

"Suit yourself," Cindy Mae said. "I'll have this ring for you by tomorrow." She tapped the printed paper.

"How much?" Will pulled the bundle of bills from his inside pocket, unable to suppress a buoyant smile.

"Cash?" Cindy Mae said, her brows raised. "Well, well. Will Adams is finally in love."

"No, Will Adams is finally putting his money where his heart is."

twenty-three

Friday night, Taylor packed. She separated her clothes into piles: California clothes and Northeast United States clothes. Claire sat on her bed, cross-legged, reading a teen magazine.

"Okay, Claire, pick what you want from this pile." Taylor motioned to the Northeast pile.

Claire poked her pretty face from behind the magazine. "Are you kidding me?" She tossed the magazine onto Taylor's desk. "This is all designer stuff, isn't it?"

Taylor anchored her hands on her hips. "Yes."

"I don't believe it." Claire picked up a cashmere sweater. Her mouth dropped open when she looked at the label. "My friends are going to die."

"Well, just don't rub their noses in it." Taylor picked a pair of slacks from the California pile and put them in her suitcase.

"Did I tell you Dad agreed to pay for half of my plane ticket when I visit you over Christmas break?"

Tears burned in Taylor's eyes. "Great. I can't wait. We'll go shopping, and you can help me replenish my wardrobe."

"You won't have to work too much will you?" Claire asked, reaching for a dark wool suit.

Taylor sighed. "Probably. But we'll have some part of the evening and weekends."

The teenager shrugged. "Would you mind if Chelle came with me?"

Taylor shook her head. "The more the merrier."

Leaving the family so close to Christmas tore at her. For the first time in years, she'd hoped to spend the Christmas season with the family, not dashing down from the city late on Christmas Eve only to leave Christmas Day after dinner.

White Birch Community Church had a Christmas play this

year, and Pastor Marlow would play Joseph. Taylor so wanted to see it.

She'd imagined staying up late after the Christmas Eve service to watch Christmas movies and drink hot chocolate with Mom.

She wanted to wake up Christmas morning and listen to her father read about the birth of Jesus from Luke's Gospel. She wanted to help Mom and Dana cook a turkey dinner and learn, finally, how to make homemade rolls.

"I'm trying this on," Claire said, dashing from the room with a red dress in her hands. "It's perfect for Christmas Eve."

Taylor answered without looking up. "Okay." She sat down on her bed, a silk blouse in her hands. Missing Christmas. It's the price she paid.

Boswell needed her, and she had a feeling *Computing Today's* article hitting the newsstands the same day she started her job was not coincidental.

It bolstered her confidence to know Boswell invested so much in her—from her salary right down to a news article.

"Besides," she said, getting up to resume packing, thoughts of Will flickering across her mind. "Other than family, there's no reason for me to stay in White Birch. None. The first day of the rest of my life begins with Boswell Global."

❧

From his chair, Grandpa watched Will pace. "You've talked to Grant, I assume."

Pensively, Will said, "Today. After I picked up the ring."

"And?"

Will faced his grandfather. "He said it was between me and Taylor, and if I could get a yes out of her, he'd be amazed. But I have his blessing and prayers."

Grandpa grinned. "He's got a point."

"I don't care. I let her get away before; if I don't ask her to marry me now, I may never get another chance."

Grandpa looked proud. "Good. You don't want to go through life wondering."

"Not about this. Not about Taylor. She's amazing, isn't she?"

"Yes, she is. Tell me, what are you going to say to her?"

Will stopped and raised his hand to lean on the mantel. "I don't know. Give her the ring—ask her to marry me." He held out his hands in question.

Grandpa cocked a brow. "That's it?"

Will pondered a minute, his chin raised. "Yeah, that's it."

Grandpa rose to his feet, chuckling. "Now look, son, I'm not a great romantic, but I've learned over the years that women like the flowery words."

Will slapped his hand to his forehead. "Flowers. Should I get flowers?"

Grandpa laughed outright. "No, no, I said flowery *words*. Tell her how you feel. Tell her what's in your heart."

"She knows how I feel."

Grandpa shook his head. "Don't tell me you need me to be your Cyrano de Bergerac."

Will furrowed his brow. "No, I don't need you to whisper sweet nothings in my ear."

"Let me remind you that the beautiful, intelligent Taylor Jo Hanson is not waiting for you to come calling. If you want her to say yes, you're going to have to bare your soul. Lay it on the line."

Will clenched and released his fists, still pacing. "You're right." He looked at Grandpa. "I know what I want. I know how I feel, but saying it in a way to win, Taylor. . .I'm going to need the help of angels."

"Well, you're in luck. I happen to know our Father in heaven commands the angels. Let's pray and ask Him for a little assistance."

"Thanks, Grandpa."

૨૦

Around nine, Claire gathered up the clothes Taylor had given her and went downstairs to watch a Christmas special with Mom. Taylor promised to join them in a minute.

She was leafing through a stack of financial periodicals

when a familiar, strong voice spoke to her from the door.

"Is someone in this room moving to California?"

She whipped around, her hand jerking to her hair and her heart beating like a runner taking off at the sound of the gun.

"Will." *I'm a mess.* "W—what are you doing here?"

"Came by to see my friend."

Her cheeks flushed when he winked at her.

"Sorry I'm such a—I mean—the room is such a mess."

His gaze never left her face. "The room is beautiful."

❧

He held out his hand. "Come on."

She slipped her hand into his. Downstairs, the family sat way too quietly in the family room. Taylor wondered what was going on as she put on her boots and coat.

"I'm going out with Will for a while," she called.

"Okay," they answered in unison.

She made a face at Will. "That's odd. Usually when they're watching a movie the house could practically burn down around them and they'd never know it."

Will opened the front door. "Who knows? It's Christmas."

Outside, the night was cold and clear. Taylor bumped Will. "What, no horse and sleigh?"

He smiled and bumped her back. "No, just you and me."

His tone sent a tingle down to her toes. When he slipped his gloved hand into hers, she wrapped her fingers around his and suddenly wanted the moment to never end.

Our last night together, she thought. Out of nowhere, her heart was overwhelmed with love for him. She tightened her jaw and pressed her lips together to keep the tears at bay.

Tomorrow night was the family Christmas dinner—weeks before the actual day—but it was their only chance to celebrate. Sunday she planned to visit New York City to say good-bye to Reneé and several of her girlfriends. Monday, she began the journey of her life.

But for now, she decided to live in the moment. "White Birch is beautiful this time of year. All the lights and decorations. . ."

"It is," Will said.

They walked several blocks toward the town square where a giant Christmas tree, much like the one in New York's Rockefeller Center, twinkled in the night.

"I watched Markie run a complete trial data conversion today. It went really well. We also reviewed the installation checklist."

He let go of her hand to put his arm around her. "Thank you. But let's not talk about business systems right now."

He made her nervous.

Suddenly Taylor heard music and found Will leading her down a path lined with dozens of glowing sand bags. "Will, what are you up to?"

Will stopped at the tall, thick Christmas tree, his pulse thundering so loudly he wondered if he'd be able to hear himself propose.

He envied ninety percent of the other men in the world who popped the question to women willing to say yes.

No guts, no glory, he thought. For the first time, he understood the depth of Taylor's devastation when she leapt out on the wings of faith and asked him to marry her.

Now the tables were turned.

"Let's have a seat." He led Taylor to the back of his truck where a thermos of hot chocolate and a pile of blankets awaited them. He opened the tailgate and helped her up.

"Did you do all this?" she murmured.

"Yes, it's your going away present." He felt cautious, afraid to reveal his hand too soon. He propped himself against the side of the truck and swept Taylor into his arms.

"You're scaring me," she said with a shaky laugh.

Will kissed her hair then rested his chin on the top of her head.

Her body stiffened. "Will, I'm leaving in three days."

He nuzzled the back of her neck. "You smell good."

"Will—" She scooted around to face him. "Please."

He cupped her face in his hands. "I love you, Taylor." He

kissed her lightly, tenderly.

When he released her, words flew out of her mouth. "Why, Will, why? Why now? Why not ten years ago? What do you want me to do with this information? Not go to California because you love me?"

"No." He resituated himself so he could retrieve the ring box from his pocket. "I don't want you to go to California because I can't live without you."

"You seem to have survived until now."

He pressed his finger over her lips. "Can I finish?"

She sucked in her bottom lip and nodded.

"You are the most incredible woman I've ever met." He looked into her green eyes. "You inspire me. You make me want to live my life better; achieve all I can achieve. Love the Lord more; love others more. I let you go ten years ago, but I can't let you leave without telling you how I feel now."

"I know how you feel." Her words landed hard, like bricks being added to a wall.

He laughed softly, the tension between them rising. "I've been praying all day about what I want to say to you."

"And?"

"I have peace. No words, just peace."

She leaned against the side of the truck and regarded him. "That's what I love most about you. The peace you exude. Not just any peace, but the peace of Jesus. I'm always so anxious."

"We'd make a good pair then."

She snarled. "Ten years ago, maybe."

"Taylor, I wouldn't have been a good husband ten years ago."

She adjusted the blanket around her legs. "Maybe I wouldn't have made a good wife."

He reached for her hand. "We loved each other. But I had grad school on my mind and wanted life to selfishly revolve around me."

"I wanted to move to New York and have a big-city career." She looked at him as a light, chilly breeze brushed through her hair. "But I like to think I would have given it up for you. I really loved you, Will."

"You would have resented me."

"Maybe." She shivered in the cold and fell against him.

"How about right now?" He wrapped her in his arms.

"What do you mean?"

He dug the ring box out of his pocket. "Would you give up California for love? For me?" He could feel her tremble. "Taylor, if you go to California, fine. But go knowing I'm yours and you are mine." He opened the box, and the ring sparkled in the glow of the candles and Christmas lights.

She gasped and covered her face with her hands.

"Taylor, marry me."

twenty-four

It wasn't supposed to be like this. Will asking her to marry him with candles and music on their last night together.

"You're kidding, right?"

Will took the ring from the box. "Does it look like I'm kidding?"

Her hand shook as she reached for the ring. "It's beautiful."

But she pulled her hand back. If she touched the jeweled piece, if she let him slide it on her finger, she'd never move to California. Never.

"Taylor?" Will turned her face to his.

She jumped off the tailgate. "What are you doing, Will? I can't marry you." With long strides, she started down the sidewalk. She stopped and whipped around. "Marry you? I'm moving in three days, Will. *Computing Today* is doing a story on me and my new job. It comes out the day I start!"

He walked toward her. "You're going to base a major life decision on a magazine article?"

"No, Will, I'm making a major life decision based on years of hard work. Am I supposed to say no to a tremendous job opportunity because Will Adams finally got his act together and asked me to marry him?" She stepped his way, hating her words but unable to cap her anger. "Ten years *too late.*"

Will grabbed her arms. "No, I'm asking you to say yes to the greatest love of your life. You may think it's ten years too late, Taylor, but our time is now."

She jerked herself free. "No, Will. No."

❧

On the west side of Kansas, weary and hungry, Taylor pulled into a small diner around seven o'clock. A light snow fell as she stepped out of the car, an empty soda cup and fast-food

166

bag wadded up in her hands. She stretched, taking a deep breath, cleansing away the fog in her mind.

She felt dull and lifeless, and dazed from the endless stretch of prairie highway. The cold evening air refreshed her, but the gentle snow reminded her of home. Of Will.

She'd cried for two days after leaving Will standing alone in the flickering lights of the White Birch Christmas tree.

Her visit with Reneé in New York centered around sobs and tissues, and ping-pong dialogue about Will's last ditch proposal.

"Sounds incredibly romantic, Taylor, but you can't pass on Boswell because Will's trying to get what he can't have," Reneé had concluded over a large slice of New York–style pizza.

Taylor shook her head. "He's not like that. If he didn't mean it, he wouldn't have asked." Then the tears had surfaced again, and Reneé handed her another tissue. "But I made a commitment to Boswell Global."

On the roof of the Kansas diner, a red-nosed, blinking Rudolph reminded her she'd be spending Christmas away from home. Mom and Dad agreed to come for New Year's, right after Claire and Chelle's visit. Taylor tossed her trash in the garbage can and stepped inside the diner. It was cozy and quaint, and she was the only customer.

A slender, gray-haired woman behind the counter greeted her. "Be right with ya, hon."

Taylor reached for a menu, her mind numb, her thoughts wandering. For the first day and a half of her journey west, she'd cried. Tears of anger—tears of heartbreak.

She'd waited ten years to hear those words from Will. She'd waited ten years to get an offer like the one from Boswell Global. "Oh, Father, I need wisdom."

"What'll it be?" the woman asked, her order pad in her hand. Her name tag read LANA.

"Diet soda and a large garden salad."

"Would you like grilled chicken or steak on the salad?"

Taylor thought for a moment. "Grilled chicken."

"You okay, honey?" Lana asked.

Taylor glanced up into a warm, friendly face. "Tired."

"Long journey."

Taylor winced at the irony. "Yes, very long."

By the time Lana brought her dinner, snow fell in big, round flakes.

"Snow's coming down pretty hard," Lana said.

Taylor smiled with a nod and picked up her knife and fork. "I'd better hurry."

"There's a motel about a mile down the road. You should stop there for the night." Lana crossed her arms and leaned against the booth.

"Thank you." Taylor wondered why Lana hung around. She was hungry and wanted to eat, but not with an audience.

"Hard decision, wasn't it?"

Taylor had just cut into her chicken. "Excuse me?"

"Hard decision—to leave love for a job."

Taylor felt the blood drain from her face. "How do you know that?"

Lana smiled as she slipped her hands into the side pockets of her uniform skirt. "The Lord spoke to me as you came in the door."

Tears burned in Taylor's eyes. "Who are you?"

Lana tugged on her name tag. "Lana Carr. My husband, Ralph, and I own this place. Been here thirty-two years."

"How do you know about my decision?"

Lana motioned to the bench across from Taylor. "May I?"

"Please." She offered her hand. "My name's Taylor."

Lana slipped into the booth. "Pleased to meet you." She shook Taylor's hand then turned and hollered across the empty dining room. "Ralph, bring me a coffee, please."

"All righty." The answer came from somewhere in the kitchen along with the clanging of pots.

"How do you know about my decision?" Taylor asked again.

Lana smiled. "I'm just a friend of Jesus, same as you."

Taylor sat back. A friend of Jesus? The notion warmed her

all over. "He told you about me?" She reached for her fork and speared a slice of chicken and tomato.

Lana rested her arms on the table. "This is our slow time of night. I pray when we hit these lulls, and I simply felt the Lord speaking to me about a woman who's torn between love and her career. I started interceding; then you walked in."

"You knew I was the one."

"I did."

Ralph came to the table with Lana's coffee. "This the young lady you've been praying for?"

"Yes. Taylor, this is my husband, Ralph."

Taylor reached up and shook his hand. "A pleasure to meet you."

"Same here," Ralph said then excused himself.

"Why did the Lord tell you about me?" Taylor asked, shoving the food around on her plate, her appetite waning.

"I wondered that myself," Lana said, holding her coffee cup and cooling the coffee with a quick puff. Taylor sipped her diet soda, studying Lana. She felt comfortable and at home with the genteel woman. She let the words flow from her heart.

"I am so torn. The job in California is an incredible opportunity. But Will Adams is an incredible man and probably the love of my life."

"And you can't have both?" Lana asked.

Taylor gave Lana a wry smile, shaking her head. "He runs a family business in New Hampshire. He can't leave."

"What about you? Do you have family in New Hampshire?"

With that question, Taylor's heart came alive. "Yes." She described her mom and dad, her brother and his family, and the beautiful pieces of fabric that made up the community quilt of White Birch.

"Sounds like a wonderful town."

"It is." Taylor took another bite of salad and washed it down with a sip of soda.

"What about this job?"

Taylor laughed, thinking of the comparison. "Work, work,

work. Lots of money. Sunshine. More work."

"A new life, eh?" Lana said.

"Sort of—more like a major career move."

Lana looked down and, from Taylor's angle, it looked like her lips moved in prayer.

After a few seconds, Lana said, "I had an opportunity many years ago to move to Hollywood and be in the movies."

Taylor's eyes widened in surprise. "Really?"

"Yes, I was one of those 'discovered' girls. Local beauty contest. You've heard the stories."

"That must have been exciting."

Lana shook her head. "I felt like the queen of the universe. Once the talent agent called me, I was knocking the dust of this little town off my feet and moving to Hollywood."

"What happened?" Taylor scooped up more salad then buttered a corner of her roll.

"That man in there happened. We were high school sweethearts. He wanted to marry me. But I refused. How could I turn down Hollywood?"

"I know," Taylor said. "That's how I feel."

Lana nodded with understanding. "Finally my wise mother pulled me aside. She said, 'Lana, it's okay to choose love.'"

Taylor sat back, her brow furrowed, the simple words "choose love" drilling into her heart. "What did that mean?"

"That if I chose to stay home and marry Ralph, that was just as wonderful as moving to Hollywood to be a star. Even more so."

"You chose love."

Lana smiled. "I did. Forty years, five children, and twelve grandchildren later, I can honestly say I've never doubted my decision."

Taylor leaned forward, wrinkling her nose. "Don't you wonder how Hollywood would have gone? Would you have become a famous star? Become rich? Lived a life of glamour?"

"Most of the girls rounded up by that agent ended up with nothing. Not one made it. A couple of them had flash fame and married rich men but wound up divorced, in custody battles—several of them were addicted to drugs and alcohol."

"Wow."

"Truth is, Taylor, I might have made it. But the Lord's will for me was right here in Kansas. Ralph built this diner, and we've led so many people to the Lord I can't count them all. It downright humbles me. Out here in the middle of nowhere, God sends us people who need His love."

"And I'm one of them."

"I suppose so."

"Oh, Lana, what do I do?"

"Tell me. Do you love him?"

Taylor lowered her head. Until now, she'd never allowed herself to ask that question. She had loved him. Past tense. But did she love him now? Present tense?

"Taylor?"

She looked up at Lana. "Yes, I love him. Very much." As soon as she said the words, peace fell over her. A sure, strong, steady peace.

"Then choose love, Taylor. Choose love."

⁂

Will dialed her cell phone for the fifth time that night. Once again, her voice mail answered. Once again, he left a message.

"I'm coming to visit you over Christmas."

Taylor left six days ago, and he'd managed short, tense conversations with her the first two days. He hadn't spoken to her since.

She'd be in California by now, but he wasn't giving up. He was keeping to Grandma's plan. Pursue her until she married someone else—or he flat grew weary. But that would take awhile.

He missed her. Everywhere he went, he thought of her. Work, the park, Peri's, the diner, church. . . In the core of his being, he knew Taylor Hanson was his wife.

"Lord, how long do I have to wait?"

Harry listened from his bed by the fireplace as Will talked

out loud. His home didn't feel like home anymore. It needed a woman's touch. It needed Taylor.

She's not even here and she's driving me crazy. He grabbed his coat and keys. "Be back later, Harry."

He drove downtown, not sure where he wanted to go or what he wanted to do. Unclipping his cell phone, he dialed Ethan.

"Are you in the mood for some of Sam's pie?"

"Not tonight. Julie's playing down in Manchester with the quartet. I'm on my way down there."

"Have a good time." Will slowed and pulled into a slot in front of the diner.

"Why don't you give Grandpa a call?"

"I just might." But there was no answer at Grandpa's, Dad's, or Bobby's, so Will decided to eat his pie alone.

Sam's was crowded. Will waved to the proprietor as he looked for a table by the fireplace. It was a cold night, and he doubted he'd find one. But as he walked toward the back, a couple vacated a table for two, and Will took their place.

A seat for me. A seat for Jesus, he thought.

Janet handed him a menu. "Eating alone tonight?"

Will grinned. "Not really."

Janet cocked a brow. "Oh, expecting someone?"

"No," Will said, trying not to laugh out loud.

Janet shook her head. "Whatever. What'll it be, Will?"

"Coffee and the biggest slice of. . ." He looked over the menu. "Apple pie a la mode."

"Coming up." She took the menu and hurried away.

Will's gaze roamed the diner. Jordan and Mia sat on the other side, deep in conversation. He was happy for them. He saw several families from church, and—oh, Grandpa and Grandma. He thought of joining them, but they looked like they were enjoying their time together.

The fire crackled behind him, and the diner's music consisted of clinking dishes and the steady murmur of voices in conversation.

He glanced toward the front door just as it opened and Taylor walked in.

His heart jumped to his throat and he couldn't breathe. Slowly, he rose to his feet.

Her eyes scanned the room as if searching for someone. When her gaze landed on him, she stormed across the diner.

"All right, all right," she said in a voice too loud.

Will moved toward her. "Taylor, what are you doing here?" He couldn't hold back a grin. Her dark hair stood on end, and her coat slipped off one shoulder and down her arm. Her designer handbag dangled from the tips of her fingers.

"There I am, halfway across the country, exhausted, crying every tear I could cry. . ."

"Do you want to sit down?" He reached for her, motioning to the other chair. Laughter bubbled from deep inside.

She jerked away from him. "No, no, I don't want to sit down."

"O—okay."

"I'm halfway across the country—I said that. Okay, I stop at this little diner to eat, out in the middle of nowhere. Nowhere, Will." Her green eyes locked on his face.

"Nowhere," he echoed.

"I finally stopped crying. I was over you. Over you."

"Over me," he said with a nod, suddenly aware of the quiet and that all eyes were on them.

"So this lady, Lana, is talking to Jesus. He tells her about me. Not me, but a woman who is choosing between love and career. Can you believe that? I never, I mean never—and she says to me, 'Choose love.' Choose love!"

Will's middle tightened with anticipation. Taylor made no sense, but he didn't care. "Love is good."

"Why did you do this to me? Why? Six days on the road and I'm still in White Birch!" She whacked his arm with her purse.

Will reached for her and pulled her to him. "What are you talking about?"

Tears streamed down her face. "I love you, Will. Always have. Always will."

He kissed her. At first tenderly then with every emotion in his heart.

The diner erupted with applause and cheers.

"All right!"

"Way to go, Will and Taylor!"

"About time!"

Taylor wrapped her arms around him and bored her head into his shoulder, weeping. "Marry me, Will. Marry me."

He stepped back and lifted her head. "No."

"What?" she asked, her expression twisted with confusion.

Slowly, Will dropped to one knee.

Taylor laughed through her tears, wiping her eyes with the back of her hand. Janet waved a napkin at Taylor with one hand, blowing her own nose with the other.

"Taylor," Will began, looking up at her, "I love you. Always have, always will. Will you marry me?"

She laughed and gripped his collar, pulling him off his knees. "Yes. Yes! I'll marry you."

He picked her up and whirled her around, laughing and hooting. When he set her down, he looked her in the eyes and kissed her with passion.

A Letter To Our Readers

Dear Reader:

In order that we might better contribute to your reading enjoyment, we would appreciate your taking a few minutes to respond to the following questions. We welcome your comments and read each form and letter we receive. When completed, please return to the following:

Fiction Editor
Heartsong Presents
PO Box 719
Uhrichsville, Ohio 44683

1. Did you enjoy reading *Lambert's Peace* by Rachel Hauck?
   ❏ Very much! I would like to see more books by this author!
   ❏ Moderately. I would have enjoyed it more if

   _____

   _____

   _____

2. Are you a member of **Heartsong Presents**? ❏ Yes ❏ No
   If no, where did you purchase this book? _____

   _____

3. How would you rate, on a scale from 1 (poor) to 5 (superior), the cover design? _____

4. On a scale from 1 (poor) to 10 (superior), please rate the following elements.

   ____ Heroine   ____ Plot
   ____ Hero   ____ Inspirational theme
   ____ Setting   ____ Secondary characters

5. These characters were special because? _____

_____

_____

6. How has this book inspired your life? _____

_____

_____

7. What settings would you like to see covered in future
   Heartsong Presents books? _____

_____

_____

8. What are some inspirational themes you would like to see
   treated in future books? _____

_____

_____

9. Would you be interested in reading other **Heartsong
   Presents** titles? ❏ Yes ❏ No

10. Please check your age range:

   ❏ Under 18   ❏ 18-24
   ❏ 25-34   ❏ 35-45
   ❏ 46-55   ❏ Over 55

Name_____

Occupation _____

Address _____

City, State, Zip_____